PUFFIN BOOKS

Warpath 1
Tank Attack

Then we crunched to a halt again and the gears screamed, metal against sand.

'Move it, Smith!' shouted Weston.

'I'm trying, sir!' I called back.

Outside the air was thick with the noise of explosions which were amplified and echoed around us inside our sweat-filled metal box. I stamped on the clutch, threw the gearbox into neutral, then quickly flicked it into first gear. I felt the engine suddenly bite and the Crusader gave another lurch forwards before it sank down. The gears whined again as the cogs spun against metal and sand.

And then it happened.

Read and collect the other books in the
Warpath *Series*

2: DEADLY SKIES
3: BEHIND ENEMY LINES
4: DEPTH-CHARGE DANGER

WARPATH 1
Tank Attack

J. ELDRIDGE

A fictional story based on real-life events

PUFFIN BOOKS

With thanks to Wing Commander Ron Finch

PUFFIN BOOKS

Published by the Penguin Group
Penguin Books Ltd, 27 Wrights Lane, London W8 5TZ, England
Penguin Putnam Inc., 375 Hudson Street, New York, New York 10014, USA
Penguin Books Australia Ltd, Ringwood, Victoria, Australia
Penguin Books Canada Ltd, 10 Alcorn Avenue, Toronto, Ontario, Canada M4V 3B2
Penguin Books (NZ) Ltd, Private Bag 102902, NSMC, Auckland, New Zealand

Penguin Books Ltd, Registered Offices: Harmondsworth, Middlesex, England

First published 1999
1 3 5 7 9 10 8 6 4 2

Set in Monotype Bookman Old Style by Rowland Phototypesetting Ltd,
Bury St Edmunds, Suffolk

Made and printed in England by Clays Ltd, St Ives plc

British Library Cataloguing in Publication Data
A CIP catalogue record for this book is available from the British Library

ISBN 0–140–38982–2

Contents

Disaster in the Desert   1
Tank Corps Uniform   4
Alamein: Opening Moves   5
Actual Rations   6

Chapter 1: First Battle   9
Chapter 2: Wounded   22
Chapter 3: Monty   30
Chapter 4: Return to the Front   35
Chapter 5: Preparing for Action   45
Chapter 6: Attack!   53

Weaponry   63

Chapter 7: Outnumbered   71
Chapter 8: Captured   83
Chapter 9: Prisoners of War   91
Chapter 10: Planning the Escape   95
Chapter 11: Break-out!   103
Chapter 12: No Way Out   110
Chapter 13: Under Attack   117
Chapter 14: Home   125

Alamein and After   130
Alamein: Rommel v. Montgomery   132
Excerpts from Tank Tips   134
Map: Allies Advance   135

Disaster in the Desert

In June 1940 Italy declared war on Britain and threatened to invade her territories in North Africa. During the summer of that year there were several skirmishes between the British 7th Armoured Division and Italian units. Then, in September 1940 the Italian army (250,000 strong) under Marshal Graziani crossed the desert and occupied key towns in Egypt (at that time a British protectorate).

Under the command of General Wavell, a British force of thirty thousand men retaliated and cut off the Italian army. There followed five months of fighting in which British, Australian and South African forces pushed the Italian infantry back, forcing them to surrender in February 1941. It looked like the Allies had won the war in the North African desert.

1

However, Hitler offered the Italian leader, Mussolini, a German armoured division to help continue the battle. The offer was accepted and shortly after the first German units arrived under the brilliant command of General Rommel – the Desert Fox, as he became known. So began a long series of battles between the Allies – including troops from Britain, Australia, New Zealand, South Africa, Rhodesia (now Zimbabwe), India and other friendly countries) and the Axis forces (Germany and Italy).

In March 1941 Rommel launched his first major offensive against the Allies. It was a success and pushed the British right back into Egypt. German forces also laid siege to Tobruk. In June, British troops under Wavell tried to break through the German defences and recover the captured town of Cyrenecia. This counter-attack failed.

During the winter many battles were fought, with the Allies losing out to Rommel and his Afrika Korps. Sensing the possibility of an unthinkable defeat, in June 1941 the British appointed Sir Claude Auchinleck as the new commander of the Allied forces, now called the Eighth Army.

In November 1941 Auchinleck mounted his

first major desert offensive: he raised the siege of Tobruk and recovered the city of Cyrenecia. This success was short-lived, as by February 1942 Rommel's forces had pushed the Eighth Army back again to the Ghazala line. Worse was to come in the summer of that year.

Rommel destroyed the Eighth Army's armour in the Battle of Ghazala and then went on to take Tobruk and to invade Egypt.

The British dug in at Alamein and managed to repel a series of German attacks. However, the situation still looked desperate. As a final throw of the dice, in August 1942 a new general was brought in, Sir Harold Alexander, along with a new commander for the Eighth Army, General Bernard Montgomery – or Monty, as he became known. Montgomery stated that there would be no more retreats: the Eighth Army would fight and win, or it would die fighting.

Our story starts in late July 1942, just before the new commanders arrive. A young tank driver prepares for action.

Tank Corps Uniform

(*As published in* Dress Regulations for the Army, 1934)

The British Army has a long tradition of a strictly enforced dress code. 'Full dress' refers to the uniform that is worn on ceremonial and formal occasions; it would never be worn in combat.

SECTION X
CORPS AND DEPARTMENTS
ROYAL TANK CORPS
Full Dress

1000. Head-dress. – A black beret, with a gilt and silver badge, with a flash in Corps colours behind. The flash is made of horse-hair in equal parts, green, red and brown, 2 inches deep, ³/₄-inch wide at the base, 1¹/₂ inches spread at the top.

1001. Tunic. – Blue cloth, the body lined drab, the skirt lined black. The collar of black velvet ornamented with ³/₄-inch gold staff lace at the top and gold Russia braid at the bottom. Black velvet pointed cuffs 3¹/₄ inches in front and 2 inches at the back, trimmed with an Austrian knot in gold wire cord, the top of the knot 8¹/₂ inches to the bottom of the cuff; eight buttons down the front. The skirt closed behind, with a three-pointed slash at each side, edged with gold wire cord and a button at each point. Twisted round gold shoulder cords, lined blue with a small button of Corps pattern at the top. Gilt and silver collar badges. Silver embroidered badges of rank.

1002. Lace. – Gold, staff pattern.

1003. Buttons. – Gilt metal with interwoven monogram "R.T.C." surmounted by a crown. For the mess dress the button is flat and the device engraved.

1004. Badges. – In silver or white metal a tank, encircled by a wreath of laurel in gilt and surmounted by the Imperial Crown. Motto "Fear Naught" in a scroll under the tank. The collar badges are in pairs.

1005. Overalls. } Blue cloth, with a black mohair staff pattern lace
1006. Pantaloons. } strips 2 inches wide down each side seam.

1007. Boots and Spurs. – As in paras. 21 and 57.

1008. Sash. – Gold and black silk web 2³/₄ inches wide; backed with black leather, two gold stripes ⁵/₈ inch wide, the rest black; round tassels of gold and a black silk fringe 8³/₄ inches long.

1009. Sword. – Infantry pattern, Appendix VI.

1010. Sword Belt. – Web, Appendix VII.

1011. Sword Slings. – Gold lace ⁷/₈-inch wide, special pattern, with a ³/₃₂-inch black silk stripe in the centre on straight grain black seal leather 1 inch wide. Flat billets, plain square gilt buckles slightly rounded at the corners.

1012. Sword Knot. – A gold and black strap, with a gold and black acorn.

1013. Gloves. – As in para. 37.

1014. Great coat. – Universal pattern, para 39.

Alamein: Opening Moves

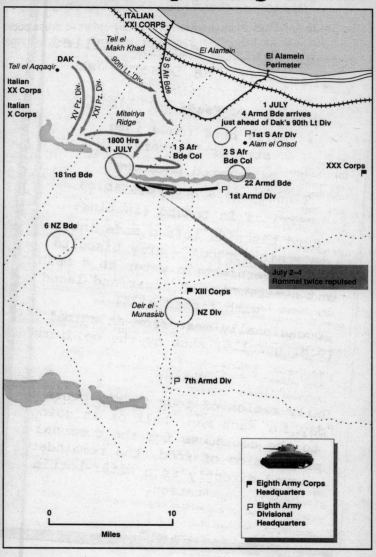

ITALIAN XXI CORPS

Tell el Makh Khad

El Alamein

El Alamein Perimeter

DAK

Tell el Aqqaqir

Italian XX Corps

Italian X Corps

XV Pz. Div.

XXI Pz. Div.

90th Lt. Div.

3 S Afr Bde

Miteiriya Ridge

1800 Hrs 1 JULY

18 Ind Bde

1 S Afr Bde Col

1 JULY
4 Armd Bde arrives just ahead of Dak's 90th Lt Div

1st S Afr Div
Alam el Onsol

2 S Afr Bde Col

22 Armd Bde

1st Armd Div

XXX Corps

6 NZ Bde

July 2–4
Rommel twice repulsed

Deir el Munassib

XIII Corps

NZ Div

7th Armd Div

0   10

Miles

■ Eighth Army Corps Headquarters

⌐ Eighth Army Divisional Headquarters

Actual Rations for the Allied Troops in the Desert War

Food:

Bully beef (made into stew or fritters)

Dehydrated potatoes

Tinned meats and vegetables

Herrings in tomato (in tins)

Hard biscuits (often made into 'Biscuit Burgoo' — army biscuits soaked overnight in water to a mush and sweetened with sugar and laced with tinned milk)

Occasionally meat from an animal (e.g. gazelle) shot by the soldiers

Water:

Daily ration of four to six pints a day for each man, half of it going to the cookhouse for the communal preparation of food, the remainder issued directly as a water-bottle ration.

I was a soldier. The desert war was long and hard. I made many friends and lost just as many. We fought for our country, we fought the enemy. I did my bit, I drove tanks. This is my story.

John Smith, Tank Driver,
Eighth Army, 1943

Chapter 1
First Battle

I'll never forget the first time I heard a
Stuka. Six of them came screaming down
from the sky at 300 mph. It was a late
afternoon towards the end of July in 1942.
I'd only spent a day at the front when
our position was attacked. Bullets from
machine-guns tore into our tents. I heard
the terrifying whine of descending bombs.
For a second I was just too shocked to
move. Then I threw myself into the shelter
of a dug-out, just as a bomb hit our
petrol dump, sending flames and thick
smoke high into the air. This was it. I was at
war.

Whistles sounded. Burning embers from
the steel drums started to rain down around
me, falling, smouldering, like a toxic hail-
storm. There was a deafening roar as the

tanks started up. And more gunfire. Some of it near, from our own anti-aircraft guns. Some, more distant: the Germans had opened fire with their big guns. Soon their Panzers would be on the horizon, launching their shells against our positions.

'Come on, Smith!' yelled Lieutenant Weston. 'Get the old girl going!'

Smith. That was me. Driver John Smith of the Tank Regiment. Nineteen years old, just arrived in the desert, and already I was about to go into battle. The 'old girl' was our tank, a Crusader. I joined the rest of the crew, ran for our tank standing in formation, and clambered up the metal side panel, using the caterpillar tracks as a ladder.

Once inside I fired up the engine. The Crusader may have been built for many things, but it wasn't designed to be comfortable. Three men – driver, radio operator and machine-gunner – squashed down below into a stinking hot metal box, with the tank commander and the gunner up in the turret. Once the hatch was closed there was even less room because the commander had to drop down into the hull.

Our radio operator, Fred Read, nicknamed Prof because everyone thought he was brainy, gave me a friendly pat on the shoulder as he slipped into his position at the back of the tank.

'Don't worry, John,' he said. 'The Germans are miles away.'

I forced a grin on to my face, though I didn't really feel like smiling. This was my first time in a real battle. True, we'd been on exercises back in England where they'd tried to make it as convincing as possible with live ammunition and exploding flares. But this was different: this was the real thing.

My stomach felt tight. I took a quick look at the faces of the other blokes in the tank with me. My new mates, Tank Crew 247. Sitting next to me was our machine-gunner, George Hoskins. He was the same age as me, although he'd been out here for three months already, so he was battle-hardened. And he looked tough. I guessed back in civvy street George must have been a boxer, or else he'd got caught up in lots of street fights, because he had old scars over his eyes and his nose had definitely been broken at some point.

Up in the turret, working the huge main gun of the tank, was Harry Atkins. Harry was older than the rest of us, about thirty years old. He was over six feet and with enormous

11

shoulders on him and built like an ox. It was his job to load the shells into the breech of the long-barrelled gun, aim, then fire.

The fifth member of our crew was our tank commander, Lieutenant Weston. Weston was twenty-three years old. He had one of these thin moustaches which a lot of the younger officers grow to make themselves look older, especially when they're commanding soldiers older than themselves.

Weston seemed all right, although I'd only met him yesterday. Harry, George and Prof seemed to respect him, so that was fine with me.

Outside the shrill blasts of the warning whistles continued, and there were crashes as the German bombs and shells hit our position with an ear-splitting roar, WHUMP WHUMP WHUMP!

Another massive explosion. The Stukas had hit a second oil dump.

German tanks were already on the horizon as I eased the Crusader forwards on its heavy caterpillar tracks. The other tanks in line were also moving up to confront the enemy.

Weston, standing above me in the turret, watched the Germans through his field-glasses. They were coming at us from all directions, straight ahead, left and right flank, trying to catch us in a pincer movement.

'Half left, driver!' barked Weston. 'Ready, gunner!'

While Harry loaded a shell into the breech, I sweated as I pulled on the left-hand steering lever, dragging the Crusader round to half left, and then set it rolling forwards. This was my first time driving a tank in the desert, and it was much harder than I'd expected. Back in England I'd driven tanks over roads and over mud and I'd got the hang of it. Driving a tank on sand was completely different, I quickly discovered. You'd be moving forwards over hard firm sand, and then suddenly you'd hit a soft patch and the tank, all twenty tons of it, would sink, and sand was much harder than mud to get a grip on.

Another twenty of our tanks were with us, heading towards the left flank.

All told there must have been a hundred enemy tanks, German Panzers by the look of them, though it was hard to tell at this distance.

'Pick your target, Atkins,' said Weston.

'Picked, sir,' answered Harry after a few seconds. 'The nearest of their tanks I can get is in my sights now.'

'OK. Fire!' said Weston.

The recoil from the gun jerked us back as if we'd been kicked by a giant boot.

I looked through my periscope. Our shell had fallen short. Not that it was easy to tell whose shell was whose, as all the other tanks in our unit were now up alongside us, firing shells at the enemy as fast as they could. Meanwhile the Germans responded with a volley of shells. One exploded about two hundred yards in front of us, showering us with sand which poured in through the hatch. Weston swiftly dropped down into the hull and pulled the hatch cover shut before we filled up with sand and choked to death.

'What can you see, Smith?' he asked.

I almost said 'sand', but Weston might have thought I was being sarkey. The truth was, sand *was* all I could see: the explosion had packed it against the mirror at the top of the periscope.

'Obscured vision, sir,' I replied.

'Then do something about it!' snapped Weston.

I jammed on the brake and let it off again. As I'd hoped this jolt made the sand drop away from the top of the periscope.

'Range to enemy closing,' I said.

'Distance?' asked Weston.

Harry spoke up. He'd been working out the range through his porthole. 'One and a half miles, sir.'

'Loaded?' asked Weston.

'All ready, sir,' said Harry.

'Then fire!' Weston shouted.

Once again the whole tank shook with the massive recoil. This time we got one: a Panzer directly ahead of us blew up. First the turret sprang away from the tank like a head knocked off a doll, then thick black oily smoke belched into the air from its engine. Finally, there was a big explosion as the fuel tank went up.

'Hit!' yelled Harry triumphantly. 'One down!'

We all cheered. George let off a short burst from his machine-gun and Prof gave Harry a thumbs-up. I had my hands full with the levers, trying to keep us out of harm's way, but I could feel a big grin of triumph sweep across my face. At that great moment even the heat and the flies didn't seem to matter. My first piece of action and we'd scored a hit.

Meanwhile the battle raged around us. Static buzzed from the radio, and then we could hear a voice crackling in Prof's headphones, though we couldn't make out what was being said. Out of the corner of my eye I saw Prof fiddling with the radio controls, trying to get a better reception, then we could hear a message come through.

'More German tanks on our right, sir! Approaching from the west,' Prof reported.

I sensed Weston pausing to think. 'Hard right, driver! Then half left. Keep it on the turn. Zigzag course, zigzag course.'

I guessed what Weston was up to: he was trying to turn us into the advancing tanks from the right so that we presented a smaller target to them. Then we'd turn again so we'd present our front to the tanks currently ahead of us. I'd done this in training. Keep moving this way and that, making a harder target to hit. Easy to do in a car, but not so easy to do in a long-based tank weighing twenty tons. Whatever we did, because of the way the Germans had come in, we'd present our long side – our vulnerable side – to one lot or the other.

I pulled the Crusader round to our right, fighting the dragging sand all the way. The controls were stiff to the touch. Maybe it was because I wasn't properly used to them. Most of the time in training we'd been driving older tanks, ones that weren't wanted so much in action. In fact the nearest tank I'd driven to this Crusader had been a Mark III, and although the controls of both tanks were similar, they were also different enough to make driving this one difficult. Especially first time out.

Above me Harry kept his gun aimed at the nearest advancing German tanks now on our left, the ones with the best chance of hitting us.

Luckily for us visibility was getting bad. The light had faded as the desert sun began its final descent behind the sand-dunes. Explosions and wind whipped sand into the air.

Suddenly the tank shuddered to a halt.

'What's happened, driver?' demanded Weston.

'I don't know, sir,' I said. 'I think some sand must have got into the gearbox, it's grinding and screaming but it won't engage.'

'Hurry it up!' grated George next to me. 'We're a sitting target here!'

I could feel myself sweating more as I tried to get the Crusader to move, but something had come apart. I could feel the gearbox fighting, feel it kicking through the control levers in my hands. Suddenly we lurched forwards, and Prof cheered, 'Yes! The boy's done it! Well done, John!'

Then we crunched to a halt again and the gears screamed, metal against sand.

'Move it, Smith!' shouted Weston.

'I'm trying, sir!' I called back.

Outside the air was thick with the noise of explosions which were amplified and echoed around us inside our sweat-filled metal box.

I stamped on the clutch, threw the gear box into neutral, then quickly flicked it into first gear. I felt the engine suddenly bite and the Crusader gave another lurch forwards before it sank down. The gears whined again as the cogs spun against metal and sand.

And then it happened.

WHUMMMPPPP! It was like being struck by a giant hammer. The enemy shell must have hit our tracks. As I looked through my periscope I saw a piece of broken caterpillar track slice towards me. Then the periscope went black.

The side of the Crusader was completely stoved in, trapping Prof. Blood poured down his face from a shrapnel wound, though where exactly he was hit it was difficult to see. Harry pulled at George, dragging him out from behind his machine-gun; it looked to me like he was out cold.

The smell of petrol suddenly filled my nostrils, mixed with a burning smell coming from Prof's position. The fuel tank! If that went up we'd all be cooked. It was every tank man's nightmare, being trapped inside a burning tank with no way out.

I clawed my way over to Prof and set to work untangling him from the wreckage of the radio, chucking things aside, radio parts, twisted bits of wire, not noticing that my hands were being burnt by the scorched metal.

'Up here!' yelled Weston's voice above me from the open hatch. I could see him and Harry leaning in through the turret. I pushed the unconscious Prof up, then Harry's powerful arms came down, wrapped themselves around Prof's chest and heaved him upwards.

The smell of burning fuel was overpowering now as the inside of the tank filled with thick choking black smoke.

'Come on, Smith! Get out!' yelled Weston.

I stumbled and cracked my head on the inside of the tank as I struggled to find the hatch opening. The smoke began to engulf me. I could feel my lungs starting to fill with fumes. I couldn't breathe, I didn't know which way was up . . . Then a hand gripped my collar and I felt myself being lifted out.

I didn't realize but the Crusader had been blown half on to its side. I tumbled down from the burning metal on to the sand below. The air was still filled with the deafening sounds of battle, the dark night sky lit up with streaks of tracer bullets, and the atmosphere heavy with the thud-thud-thud of tank and anti-tank weapons battling it out.

The sleeves of my uniform smouldered from where I had dragged Prof from the burning metal. I dropped to my knees and poured handfuls of sand over my smoking sleeves to put them out. My hands and forearms were black, though whether from smoke or oil, or whether they were burnt, I didn't know. I could hardly feel them, which wasn't a good sign.

'Come on, let's get out of here!' yelled Harry, and he started to pull me away from the tank. My knees dragged against the sand, tearing off more skin. Then the whole desert around me suddenly exploded. I flew through the air. WHUMP! For a split second there was silence, followed by a terrible pain in my head and then . . . nothing.

Chapter 2
Wounded

There was a grey film over my eyes. Smoke?
No, not smoke. Something else. I didn't know
what it was. My eyelids felt sticky. I was having difficulty opening them. My head thumped
with a dull ache.

There was a buzzing sound. A bell? No. A
fly, settling on my face.

I tried to brush it off with my hands but
they felt heavy and clumsy.

A voice called: 'This one's awake!'

This time I managed to open my eyes
and looked around. I was in a field hospital.
My hands and arms were bandaged. A
medical officer stood over me. He studied
me for a second or two, then held up two
fingers.

'How many fingers can you see?' he asked.

What a strange question! I thought.

'Two,' I said.

'Good,' the MO nodded, putting his hand down. 'After that knock on the head we thought you might have double vision.' He bent down to examine my head, and then I became aware of the thick bandages wrapped round it like a helmet.

'You were lucky,' he commented. 'You obviously have a very thick skull.'

Daylight filtered into the huge tent. It was very hot. The flies were everywhere, despite the mosquito nets. Another one of them began crawling over my face and again I tried to swat it away, but it was impossible, strapped up as I was like an Egyptian mummy.

As I lay there it gradually came back to me what had happened.

'Are the others OK?' I asked.

'They'll live to fight another day,' said the MO. 'So will you.'

There was a shout from another part of the tent, an orderly calling for him to come and take a look at a patient.

'Coming!' replied the MO. To me he said: 'Don't worry, we'll soon have you back in action again.' With that he went.

My head still ached. I felt awful. I felt responsible for what had happened.

'How you feeling, John?' said a familiar voice.

I forced my head round and saw that Prof was lying on the next bed, with a leg bandaged up. He grinned.

'Thanks, mate,' he said. 'You saved my life.'

'It was my fault in the first place,' I said miserably. 'If I hadn't stalled the tank . . .'

'Don't blame yourself,' said Prof. 'Those tanks are always breaking down.'

Despite what Prof said I still felt guilty. My first outing into battle and I'd messed it up. Worse, because of me Prof was lying injured in the hospital tent.

'How are the others?' I asked.

'They're all OK,' Prof reassured me. 'George got a bang on the head, but he's all right now. You and I are the only ones from our crew who ended up here.'

'Shut up talking, you two!' snapped the orderly. 'There're sick people here trying to get some sleep!'

Prof winked at me.

'It's a great life in the army, innit?' he grinned.

I did my best to smile.

24

Next day I was able to get up, though my hands, arms and head were still heavily bandaged. Prof had to stay in bed, his ankle had been badly twisted, though nothing broken, luckily for him.

In the afternoon, Lieutenant Weston called in to see how we were. I could hardly look him in the face, I felt so guilty about stalling the tank and getting us blown up.

'I'm sorry, sir,' I said.

'Sorry for getting injured?' asked Weston.

'For stalling the tank, sir,' I said.

'It wasn't your fault, Smith,' said Weston. 'The engineers had a look at it, what's left of it. It was the gearbox. Sand had got in and clogged it up so it couldn't engage properly. The best driver in the world wouldn't have made that tank move.'

That made it a bit better, but I still felt bad about what had happened.

'The other lads think you're a bit of a hero, saving Read like that. And on your first engagement, as well. Well done, Smith. We're proud to have you on our crew.'

That was as maybe, but I'd been the driver and we'd been hit because the engine had stalled.

After Weston had gone, I sat by Prof's bed

and we played draughts. Whether it was because I had difficulty moving my pieces with bandaged hands, or whether it was just that Prof was a better player, he beat me, eight games to one. As we played we talked, and I learnt more about the rest of Crew 247.

Our huge, strong gunner, Harry Atkins, had been a blast furnace stoker at a steel mill in the north of England – a place called Consett. That explained the scars on his forearms. According to Prof, everyone who works in a steel mill has scars from bits of molten metal splashing as it's poured into the moulds.

I'd been right about George Hoskins having been a boxer. According to Prof, when he'd been called up George had been the Amateur Middleweight Champion of North London, with the prospect of going all the way as a professional. Prof also had a high regard for Weston.

'He won't shy away from a fight, but he won't take stupid chances,' said Prof. 'There are too many good men who've died out here in the desert because their tank commander was after that little bit more glory than the others and did something crazy, like charging after the enemy on his own. Not that Weston had been removed from his command and a new overall commander, General Alexander, was overseeing the whole Middle East operation. And some general called Montgomery had been put in charge of the Eighth Army.

'I thought General Gott was going to take over the Eighth,' said Prof. 'At least, that's what everyone was saying.'

'He was, but the plane Gott was in was shot down a couple of days ago and he was killed, so now they're bringing out this Montgomery from England,' said the orderly. He sighed. 'Another general. The way this war's going we'll get through a dozen more of them before it's over.'

I had to agree – it wasn't looking too clever.

Chapter 3
Monty

Prof and I spent the next two weeks in hospital. Back at the front the battle raged, with many casualties and neither side getting anywhere. Lieutenant Weston came over once to let us know that Tank Crew 247 had been given a captured Italian tank to use until the proper replacement tanks arrived. Things went on much the same, day after day. Then, about the middle of August, panic hit the hospital, with doctors, nurses and orderlies rushing around packing things away: instruments, loose mosquito nets, anything that wasn't fixed down.

'What's going on?' I asked an orderly. 'Are we retreating?'

'Monty's coming,' snapped the orderly, and then rushed off.

I looked across at Prof.

30

'Monty?' I asked, puzzled.

'General Montgomery,' said Prof. 'He's obviously arrived sooner than people thought.'

'Inspecting a field hospital?' I frowned. 'Why?'

'From what I've heard about Monty he's that sort of general,' said Prof. 'He's a soldier's soldier. He likes to know what all his men think. Also, he wants to let them know that he's there to fight with them, not from some base far away from the action.'

About two hours later the man himself arrived. Those of us who could walk were ordered to stand beside our beds. There was a grinding of brakes outside the tent and the sounds of boots crunching on the sand as the guards on duty stamped to attention. We heard the sounds of voices outside our tent welcoming our new commander, and then suddenly he was there among us. Monty himself. Lieutenant General Bernard Montgomery, commander of the whole Eighth Army. He was shortish with a thin pointed face and a tiny moustache. What I particularly noticed was the black beret he wore on his head. It was a tank commander's beret, with the Royal Tank Regiment badge. The new commander was a tank man, one of us.

Monty did a quick tour of inspection, moving swiftly from bed to bed, asking a question now and then of the doctors, saying a few words of encouragement to some of the men who were still in bed.

When he got to me he stopped, looked up at me and read my name tags.

'Smith,' he said.

'Yes, sir,' I said, still standing stiffly to attention.

'I hear you performed a heroic act, Smith,' he said. 'Pulling your fellow crew-member from a burning tank. That was a very brave act. This army could do with more men like you. Well done.'

I was stunned. Speechless. Here was the commander of the whole Eighth Army, just arrived out here in Africa, and complimenting me – an ordinary private – on getting Prof out of the tank. From the urgent expression on the face of the medical officer standing just behind Monty, I realized that I was expected to say something in reply. Not knowing what else to do, I saluted with my bandaged hand and said:

'Thank you, sir. I'm proud to be in the Eighth Army.' Then wished I'd said something more original.

'Good man,' said Monty.

With that he moved on to the man in the next bed.

I still felt stunned. Prof, also standing to attention as best he could on crutches, gave me a quick grin.

After his inspection, Monty went to the door of the hospital tent, then turned and addressed us all.

'Men!' he said. 'It is a privilege for me to be here with you in the desert. I come here with express orders from the prime minister himself, Winston Churchill. These orders are very simple. We are to push Rommel and his forces out of North Africa. There will be no more retreats by the Allied forces. Very shortly we are going to advance from Alamein. Once we begin there will be no turning back. We are going to fight and we are going to win. The people back home are depending on us. I will not let you down. I know you will not let the people back home down.'

With that, Montgomery left the hospital tent, heading off on the next part of his whistle-stop tour of inspection of the Allied lines.

After Montgomery had gone, Prof came over to me, grinning broadly now.

33

'So,' he said, 'Crew 247 has its own hero.'

'Shut up,' I said, feeling embarrassed. 'I don't feel like one – just the opposite. Anyway, it wasn't just me. Weston and Harry pulled you out as well.'

'Yeah, but you've got the injuries,' said Prof. 'That makes you the hero.' He turned and look out through the tent flap at Monty's car as it sped off across the desert, leaving a cloud of sand in its wake.

'D'you think he means it?' I asked. 'About us not retreating any more.'

Prof nodded. 'I think he does,' he said. 'From now on it's going to be fight, or die fighting. Dig in and fight. Whatever, it looks like Alamein's going to be where it all happens.'

Chapter 4
Return to the Front

A couple of days after Monty's visit the MO told me and Prof that we were being discharged and returned to the front. This was fine as far as we were concerned. We both felt frauds sitting here in the hospital when our wounds were nearly healed.

We grabbed a ride back to our regiment on a truck that was taking a load of other blokes back to Alamein. Most of them were returning to the front after four days' leave in Cairo.

We got back to the new base camp. Then Prof and I set off to find Tank Crew 247. Our unit had taken up a position on the ridge, on the front line at El Alamein. From the state of the tanks, our forces had taken a hammering in the last few weeks: busted caterpillar tracks, scorched and dented armour all over the place.

We found Lieutenant Weston first. We stood smartly to attention in front of him and saluted.

'Driver Smith and Radio Operator Read reporting for duty, sir!'

Weston grinned.

'At ease,' he said. 'Good to have you both back. How are the arms, Smith? And you, Read? How's the leg?'

We assured him that we were both fit enough to return to duty.

'Good,' he said, 'because we've got the new tank. It arrived yesterday. A Grant. Think you can handle it?'

A Grant! This was great news! The Grant was the Medium Tank M3, American-made. I'd heard about it but never actually seen one. There were two sorts of M3 tank: the Lee, which was the standard version, and the Grant, which had been made to British specifications. Although the Grant wasn't that much different from the Crusader, the two things in its favour were its heavier armour and, for me as the driver, the fact that it was reckoned to have much better manoeuvrability.

The Grant had a crew of six, compared to the Crusader's five-man crew. I wondered who our extra man was? We found out when we followed Weston to the tank lines. Teddy and Harry were at work, making their own modifications to the Grant. With them was a young lad.

'Smith and Read, meet Private White, our new crew-member,' said Weston. 'He's our machine-gunner and co-driver. He used to be with Crew 533, until they lost their tank and most of their crew.'

I gave White a sympathetic look.

'Tough luck,' I said.

'It wasn't too clever,' he replied. 'Only one of us was killed. The others were wounded. I was lucky, I suppose. I came out with just a scratch on my arm.'

Weston looked at his watch. 'Right,' he said, 'there's a briefing for all tank commanders. I'll report back the top brass's intentions as soon as we've finished. In the mean time, carry on getting her into shape. You'd better take her for a spin, Smith, to get used to the controls.'

With that Weston went, heading for the command tent.

'Welcome back,' grinned George. 'Ready for some action after all that rest?'

While we worked to get the Grant ready,

Prof and I learnt a bit more about our new crew-member.

Fred White was seventeen. Like nearly everyone else named White in the army, he was known as Chalky, but he didn't mind. He seemed a nice enough young bloke, tall and thin, a bit like George, with his black hair almost shaved to the roots. Army barbers often did that to new recruits. They said it stopped you getting lice out in the tropics, but I reckon they just enjoyed cutting everyone's hair off. Chalky came from Birmingham and had worked in a munitions factory up there, so he already knew a bit about weapons before he joined up. He'd been out here for two months as a co-driver and machine-gunner before his tank had been blown up. Although he was a quiet lad, a bit shy, once you got him talking about weapons he could talk forever about them. A bit like me and engines and Prof and radios, I suppose. We all talk a lot about the things we're most interested in.

Because the Grant had a crew of six, there'd been some changing round of jobs to fit Chalky in. Harry would continue to load the main gun, but George would now actually aim and fire it. This way, with both of them working together, we'd get a faster rate of fire. That was another advantage of the Grant over the Crusader.

Prof and I walked around the new tank, inspecting it, while George, Harry and Chalky told us all the good points about it.

'Twenty-six miles an hour on a good surface,' said Harry. 'It can go up a sixty-degree gradient, and clear any obstacle two feet high. It can cross a trench six feet wide.'

'What's the armour like?' I asked.

'Riveted steel, up to two inches thick in parts,' replied George. 'Great protection!'

Again, a bit thicker than the armour on the Crusader.

'Tell them about the armaments, Chalky,' said Harry. He grinned at us. 'Chalky's a whizz on guns. Nearly as clever as Prof on anything technical.'

Chalky patted the hull of the tank, like he was proud of it already.

'The main gun in the right-hand hull is a 75 mm, with gyro-stabilizing elevation.'

'In other words, you can fire it on the move,' added George. 'Greater control.'

Chalky indicated the machine-guns poking out.

'In the front is a 37 mm M5 L/50 with 178

rounds. Plus a Browning M1919A4 machine-gun, with another two in the bow and one AA.'

Not bad, I thought.

'The turret's hydraulically operated and can turn a full circle,' put in Harry. 'We can swing the turret round faster, and right round if we need to. All in all, we can fire faster and we can move faster.'

'And we're calling her Bessie,' said George proudly.

Harry, George and Chalky walked us round to the front where, in white letters, George had painted the name 'Bessie' on her. She was the top of the range. The best. And she was ours.

Prof and I jumped up on to the hull. Then I clambered down into the driver's compartment while Prof climbed up to the turret and slipped down through the hatch, into the radio operator's seat.

That was the first difference with the Grant: the driver and co-driver sat at the front of the tank in a separate compartment from the rest of the crew. Chalky and I would be communicating with Weston, and the rest of the crew in the main compartment, through headphones and throat microphones.

As I sat I ran my hands over the steering

levers, checking them for ease of movement.

There was no doubt about it, Bessie was a beauty. The Grant had obviously been built by people who knew what a tank had to do, and how difficult some of the earlier tanks had been to operate.

George leapt up beside me.

'Remember what Weston said, take her for a run,' he said. 'See how she works out.' He grinned at me. 'After all, he'd rather you knew what you were doing with her before you go into battle, than get something wrong in the middle of it.'

Although I knew he was only joking, I didn't smile back. Weston and Prof had said that the tank stalling wasn't my fault, but I still didn't feel happy about what had happened. I didn't want anything going wrong next time. I needed to feel confident on my handling of the tank I was driving, especially with a brand-new one like the Grant. Like Weston had said, I had to test it out. It's the same with anything that moves: it may look absolutely perfect, but the only real test of a vehicle is to drive it.

I nodded at George. Then I called to Prof, 'Are you OK in the back, there? I'm going to put her through her paces!'

Prof's reply came to me through the headphones, but I couldn't hear him properly. I'd forgotten about the intercom. I picked up the headphones and throat microphone set and put them on.

'Smith to Read, come in,' I said.

'Hearing you loud and clear,' came Prof's voice. 'No need to shout any more, John. This is a great system. Not only are we connected with base camp, but we've got intercoms. Great stuff!'

'D'you fancy going for a ride?' I asked him.

'OK by me,' said Prof. 'I can check the set for vibrations when mobile. Let her go.'

George dropped down from the hull and I started Bessie up. The engine was noisy, but not as noisy as some tanks. I set it moving forwards, nice and slow. When you're first getting used to a new tank you don't want to go too fast.

I pulled back on my right-hand lever and turned Bessie right, out of the line, and moved her along behind the row of tanks in front of us. She turned beautifully. Mind, the sand was firm and level. I wondered how she'd cope with soggy sand.

'Smith to Read,' I said into my microphone.

'How you doing, Prof? Over.'

'Read to Smith,' came Prof's voice in my ears. 'Stabilizers working perfectly. All systems operational.'

I put Bessie through her paces for about half an hour, checking visibility, how she manoeuvred, lever actions, foot-pedal stiffness – all the sort of things you need to feel confident with before you take a tank into battle. Visibility was better because vision was direct: a window in a hatch in front of you. The hatch could even be opened for improved vision.

I took her out on to the open desert, although still inside our defence barriers, and brought her up to speed. Then I tried a few skid-turns, first to the left, then to the right, each time easing back on the lever and guiding her into the line of the skid. It's the sort of thing you can only do on firm sand, or gravel, or a greasy surface. Try it on soft sand and one side of the tank just sinks down and you get stuck.

Bessie responded well to everything. She was a good tank. I brought her back to our place in the line and climbed down, just as Weston appeared.

'I hope you've been careful with that tank,

43

Smith,' he said with a grin. 'We're going to need it.'

We all looked at him inquisitively.

'We've just been given our orders,' he announced. 'We're going on the offensive.'

Chapter 5
Preparing for Action

We all thought that meant we were going into battle straight away, but that wasn't to be the case. Weston briefed us on Monty's long-range attack plan.

'He wants Rommel's forces weakened before we launch our next big attack,' he said. 'Apparently Rommel's weak spot is his supply line. Because the Axis forces have pushed forward at such a speed, their front-line troops are a long way from their depots. Monty reckons that Rommel needs a quick victory because his stocks of fuel and ammunition must be running low. It takes a long time for his supplies to arrive because of the distance his trucks have to travel across the desert. So, the longer we can hold out here at Alamein, the better it is for us.

'The plan is to keep the Germans at bay

while the RAF mount bombing raids on the truck convoys. Obviously some of their supplies will get through, but by the time our big push comes, Monty reckons the German forces will be low on ammunition and fuel.

'So, our orders are to sit tight, keep the enemy busy, keep alert, and be ready for the big one when it comes.'

And so we waited. For two months a series of battles raged around our positions at Alamein and the ridge at Alam el Halfa. Up to the end of August, right through September and into October. At the beginning of September Rommel's tanks launched a huge attack against our lines at Alam el Halfa, but the Eighth Army defended so fiercely that the Axis forces had to retreat. Then, early in September, our New Zealand division launched a counter-attack to the west of us. This time the Axis forces defended strongly, and our boys were forced to retreat. That was the way it went for the whole of those two months: attack and counter-attack, again and again and again.

Then, on 23 October came the orders for the big assault. Weston briefed us on our role.

'This is it, men,' he told us. 'We're going forward. The long-range artillery are going to open with a barrage on the enemy positions at 2140 hours. At the same time four divisions of infantry – the 1st South Africans, 2nd New Zealand, 9th Australian and the 51st Highlanders – will start moving forwards, using the barrage as our cover. The sappers will clear a path through the minefields so our tanks can get through. It's reckoned it'll take them some time. After all, they've got to get through the barbed wire, find and clear the mines, and then mark a tank path for us. The estimated time for our tanks to start moving is 0200 hours.'

Weston checked his watch. 'Right, it's now 1600 hours. I'll see you all back here at 2100 hours so we can make final preparations. In the mean time I suggest you all get some rest. It's going to be a long night, chaps.'

With that, Weston left and headed for his tent.

'We've got five hours,' said Harry. 'I'm going to get some kip. Anyone else?'

We shook our heads.

'I don't see how you can sleep at a time like this!' I said. 'We're about to go into battle!'

'I can sleep because I'm older than you lot,' said Harry. 'I've seen it all before. And I need my rest. See you later.'

And with that, off he went.

'I'm going to the mess – get something to eat,' said George. 'Anyone coming with me? Fancy a cuppa or something, John? Chalky?'

Chalky shook his head. He looked even paler than before. He was probably remembering the last time he went into battle – when he'd only just made it through. I supposed he was wondering if he'd be so lucky this time.

'No,' he muttered. 'I think I'll just check the guns over.'

'Much better to come to the mess tent,' said Prof.

'I just don't feel hungry,' said Chalky.

'Nor do I,' said Prof, 'but it's better to relax. Have a cup of tea and talk.'

'Come on,' I said, and I slapped Chalky on the shoulder. 'Let's go and unwind.'

The mess tent was full, mostly with tank crews making sure they got a meal before the action started. Once the action began you never knew when you'd next get a chance to eat.

Everyone knew someone who'd been killed

in this war, and so everyone was aware that for them this could be their last few hours.

'At least we're protected,' said Prof. 'I mean, we've got armour around us. The ones I feel sorry for are the blokes in the infantry – out there with just a gun and a bayonet and a tin hat.'

'Each to his own,' said George. 'Me, I wouldn't like to be up in a plane. At least if we get hit we can jump out. If a plane gets it the pilot hasn't got much chance.'

'They've got parachutes,' pointed out Prof. 'They can bail out.'

'And land right on the enemy,' laughed George. 'Or in a tree. Or in a river. No, you've got no proper control with a parachute.'

'My dad didn't want me to join up,' said Chalky suddenly. 'He fought in the First World War. He said seeing what he saw put him off fighting for life. We had a row when I first told him I was joining up.'

'That's understandable,' I said.

'My mum was on my side, though,' added Chalky.

He fell silent, obviously thinking about home. About his dad and his mum.

'What's it like where you live?' I asked. I could tell he needed to talk.

49

'It's all right,' he said. 'It's all factories. That's what Birmingham is. Factories. And rows and rows of houses. I had a letter from my mum just before I came out. They were being bombed. It was terrible. She reckoned it was because our house is so close to the factories.'

'Same thing for me,' said George. 'My mum wrote and said she's worried about how the bombing's affecting my Uncle Jim's pigeons.'

'His pigeons?' asked Prof.

George nodded. 'He keeps racing pigeons,' he said. 'On his roof.' He laughed. 'I ask you, all this bombing going on, people and houses getting blown up, and my mum's worried about a load of pigeons!'

'My mum cooks pigeons,' said Chalky. 'She makes them into pies. She said meat's hard to get hold of, so she gets my little brother to catch what he can and she turns it into stews and pies. Pigeons. Rabbits.'

'I bet anyone who's got a cat or dog in your street keeps it indoors when your little brother's about!' George chuckled.

We all joined in laughing, thinking of Chalky's mum making pies out of people's pets.

And so it went on, just talking to pass the

time, filling in the silences. I could tell that it helped Chalky to hear us talk and find out that we were all as nervous as him.

We whiled the next few hours that way, and at 2100 hours, we went back to Bessie, our new Grant. Weston was already there. Harry joined us soon after, looking refreshed from his sleep. Many of the other crews had also arrived early to carry out last-minute checks on their tanks. We checked everything twice, then a third and final time: the caterpillar tracks, the guns, the ammunition, the radio, the steering, the hatch opening mechanism, every last nut and bolt. By the time the whistle went to assemble, all the crews were there, ready and waiting by their tanks.

I looked at my watch: 21.39. One minute to go. Although we weren't due to get involved in any action ourselves until 0200, we knew that once the barrage started, we were committed.

21.39 and 59 seconds . . .

As my watch showed 2140 hours, the barrage from the big guns just behind us started up. There was a crescendo of noise as we heard WHOOOMP WHOOOMP WHOOOMP with shell after shell sent on its way to the

51

distant enemy positions, the sand vibrating beneath us.

This was it.

Chapter 6
Attack!

The barrage continued as 1,000 big guns hammered and pounded the enemy positions, the shells soaring over our heads. The area ahead of us was now blazing with light from the bursting shells. Every now and then one of the explosions of white light would be accompanied by a flare of red, flame and smoke, as a shell struck a target, though at this distance it was impossible to see clearly what had been hit.

Ahead in the distance, through the smoke, I saw the sappers come out from the slit trenches in our defensive box and move forwards. Prof's comments about the foot soldiers earlier had been right. I didn't envy their job, going out against enemy artillery and tanks with just a steel helmet for protection. We were protected inside our tank.

Out there the sappers had no protection. And the job they had to do was dangerous. They had to clear the mines along pathways wide enough for us to use.

Behind the sappers I could see the infantry emerging, dressed in shorts and cardigans, rifles with bayonets attached at the ready. They were as unprotected from enemy shells as the sappers. They began their advance, following the sappers, heading towards the enemy lines.

At certain points searchlights directed their beams straight up into the sky to help them see the correct path to follow. Light anti-aircraft guns, too, fired tracer shells at intervals in the right directions, all intended to show them the way forward.

The barrage continued relentlessly. For the next hour the night desert was rocked by heavy fire and lit up by lights and gunfire. The infantry were out of sight from us now, disappeared into the smoke. More time passed. We couldn't see what was going on, all we could do was listen, and wait. Midnight came and went. Then one o'clock. Finally, after what seemed like a whole night of waiting, our orders came to 'Mount up!' (a leftover from the days when horses were the only transport used by the army), so we got on board.

I settled into the driver's seat, with Chalky next to me. The other four clambered down through the turret hatch into the body of the tank: Prof first, then George and Harry, and finally Lieutenant Weston took his command position in a seat at the top of the turret.

'OK?' I asked Chalky. He nodded and forced a grin.

'You're in safe hands with our commander,' I said. 'Weston's a good bloke.'

We put on our headsets and heard Weston's voice coming out through the earphones, testing our connections one at a time. In turn we responded through our throat mikes:

'Driver, come in.'

'Reading you, sir. Over.'

'Co-driver, come in.'

'Reading you, sir. Over.'

On through the rest of the crew. Then Prof patched in to base communications, responding to their question.

'Crew 247, are you receiving? Over.'

'Crew 247 reading you loud and clear. Over.'

And so it went on down the rest of the line,

along all the other tanks: the other Grants, the Valentines, the Stuarts, the Crusaders. Everyone was waiting. Finally, at 0200 hours, came the order: Forwards!

I eased Bessie into the line of tanks and we began our course through our own defensive minefields in single file. Once we'd cleared our own positions we carried on across the two miles of no man's land, and then into the tank-path through the enemy minefield cleared for us by the sappers.

Once we were clear of the tape markers and into enemy territory, the tank directly ahead of us began a half-turn and I followed suit. This left the way clear for the tank behind us to move ahead into my space. The tank ahead of me went wider, and I straightened up again. I nosed forwards, and now we were all in a line, headed for the enemy.

'Put a round into the breech,' said Weston.

'Ready, sir,' came Harry's voice. There was the sound of a large shell being slipped into the breech, the sound of metal on metal echoing through to Chalky and me in our front compartment. I kept Bessie rolling.

'Fire!' snapped Weston.

George fired the big gun, and from that moment we were in action. All along the line the other tanks opened fire, shell after shell. And now the enemy responded. Ahead of us there were flashes as their field guns and tanks opened fire. The desert around us began to shake as their shells hit. Out of the corner of my eye I saw a brilliant flash of light to my right and Bessie shook violently, then recovered. The Grant immediately to our right had taken a direct hit. I kept rolling forwards.

'Pick up some speed, Smith,' said Weston. 'Put some space between us and their shells.'

'Sir,' I said.

I opened the throttle and increased the speed to twenty-five miles an hour. Weston was hoping that the field guns of the Axis forces would be calculating our speed at fifteen miles an hour, dropping their shells accordingly. Although we were now getting nearer to the enemy, his theory was that we would be travelling faster than they guessed and so their shells would fall behind us. It was a good theory, provided we didn't get hit by shells falling short.

George and Harry were obviously working like clockwork together because Chalky and I could hear each shell being loaded into the breech followed by the huge crash of the main gun being fired at regular and fast intervals.

Suddenly the sky ahead of us was lit up by flares bursting bright above the Axis positions, illuminating them clear as daylight. The RAF had started their attack. Tracers of machine-gun and anti-aircraft fire poured upwards into the sky from the Axis positions, trying to bring down the planes overhead. We continued shelling the enemy positions.

Over my earphones I heard Prof say: 'Copy that. Over and out.' He had obviously received instructions from HQ.

'Orders from base, sir,' Prof said, all of us hearing his voice in our phones. 'Take a direction due east. Panzer division approaching.'

Our planes had spotted a counter-attack coming from the German positions.

'Due east, Smith,' said Weston.

'Aye, sir,' I said.

I eased the right-hand lever back and swung Bessie round, checking the compass and turning until I had an easterly direction. I saw four other tanks doing the same. I guessed there were others joining us. We had obviously been chosen as the group to confront the oncoming Panzers.

By now it was past three o'clock in the morning. The battle had been raging for over five hours, ever since our big guns had begun their barrage. We left the rest of our tanks to continue their advance towards the Axis positions while our group headed due east across the open desert.

A double note in my earphones told me that a radio transmission was coming in. Then I heard Prof's voice responding with 'Received' and 'Copy' and 'Over and out.' We soon learned what it was all about when he relayed it to Weston and we picked up their conversation over our headsets.

'Captain Mason of Tank Crew 333 presents his compliments, sir,' said Prof. 'He's been detailed by HQ to take charge of this squadron.'

'Tell Captain Mason we are happy to oblige,' said Weston. 'What are his orders?'

'Crew 333 will take point position. We are to proceed at his speed in convoy behind him until he gives the order to stop. Douse all lights. No firing. He says he doesn't want to alert the enemy to our position. He says there's a ridge about nine miles ahead which will give us cover. We will lay in an ambush for the enemy there.'

'Acknowledge,' said Weston.

Prof relayed Weston's message back to the radio operator of Crew 333. For the next half an hour we travelled at roughly twenty miles an hour over the desert sand. To our left and behind us the fighting continued with flares and explosions. Even at this distance from the battle, the sand shook and the desert echoed as the heavy guns of both sides crashed out their shells. We slid silently through the night in single file, with just the sound of the engine beating, our gear wheels clonking and grinding, and our caterpillar tracks swishing over the sand.

The radio crackled into life again, and then Prof once more relayed the instructions from Captain Mason in Tank 333: 'Halt.'

I eased on the brake and brought Bessie to a stop. We sat there with the engine idling.

'Captain Mason's orders,' said Prof. 'Take up position to the right of the ridge ahead.'

'To the right of the ridge ahead,' acknowledged Weston.

I pulled Bessie round and headed for our new position. The tank behind me did the same, coming up alongside me. Soon all eight tanks were in place, four at each side of the high ridge, our guns trained on the dip in the ridge where the Panzers would be expected to come through. Now all we could do was sit there and wait.

'I hate this waiting,' Harry's voice grumbled through my headphones.

'You'll be in action soon enough,' replied Weston smoothly.

The radio crackled again, then Prof reported to us: 'Captain Mason's going out to take visual observation.'

We saw the hatch of Tank 333 open, then the figure of Captain Mason climb out and drop down. He made his way up the high ridge, crouching low all the time. When he got near the top he dropped on to his front and crawled the last few feet to the top. From my open hatch I could see him raise his binoculars to his eyes, then scan the desert ahead. On the eve of a full moon, visibility wasn't bad. Mason lay like that for a moment or two, then he got up quickly and slid back down the ridge. He looked like a man in a hurry.

Having raced back to his tank, he dropped down into the turret and pulled the hatch shut after him. A few seconds later we heard Prof on the radio receiving an incoming message.

Prof relayed the news to Weston: 'Captain Mason's compliments, sir, but he says we've got a spot of bother. He says either the RAF boys underestimated just how big the Panzer

61

division is that we've been sent to intercept, or the Germans decided to increase it after it was spotted.'

'Give us the bad news, Read,' said Weston. 'How many of them are there?'

Prof hesitated before replying: 'Captain Mason estimates about fifty Panzers heading this way. They should be at the ridge in about five minutes.'

We all let this sink in. Fifty Panzers against eight of us. We were outnumbered by more than six to one. Weston was silent for a moment, then he asked Prof: 'Does Captain Mason have any orders about what our tactics should be?'

'Yes, sir,' said Prof. 'He's radioed our situation back to base. In the mean time he orders us to continue as before. He's working out a plan for a delaying action until reinforcements arrive.'

It had taken us hours to get to this point from HQ. Our nearest support tank unit was over an hour away, and it would be engaged in the big battle going on behind us.

We all fell silent as we weighed the situation up. It would be at least two hours before any reinforcements arrived, and fifty enemy tanks would be upon us in less than five minutes.

WEAPONRY
Crusader Mark III

Specification
Crew: 5
Engine power: 340 bhp
Combat weight: 44,287 lb (20,085 kg)
Max speed: 26.70 mph (43 km/h)
Length: 19.67 ft (5.994 m)
Range: 124.2 miles (200 km)
Width: 8.67 ft (2.642 m)
Main gun: 6-pounder (57 mm)
Height: 7.33 ft (2.235 m)
Armour: 0.28—1.93 in (7—59 mm)

The Crusader, manufactured by the British company
Nuffields, was the main tank of the Eighth Army
during the Desert War. Over 5,300 were produced.
The Mark I was rushed into production without
thorough testing and was mechanically unreliable.
Its 2-pounder (40 mm) gun was easily outclassed,
and the small machine-gun in a turret on the
front hull was found to be unnecessary. This
machine-gun was removed on the Crusader Mark II,
but only on the Mark III was the main armament
upgraded to a 57 mm, 6-pounder, which allowed it
to fight German armour on equal terms.

Grant

Specification
Crew: 6
Engine power: 340 bhp (253.64 kW)
Combat weight: 60,604 lb (27,240 kg)
Max speed: 26.08 mph (42 km/h)
Length: 18.50 ft (5.64 m)
Range: 119.85 miles (193 km)
Width: 8.92 ft (2.718 m)
Main gun: 2.96 in (75 mm)
Height: 10.25 ft (3.124 m)
Armour: 0.50—2.25 in (12.7—57 mm)

The Grant was the name given by the British
to the American-made Medium Tank M3, which
was developed by mounting a 75 mm gun on
the right-hand side of a modified M2
(light) tank. British combat experience in
North Africa highlighted the disadvantage
of the M3's limited traverse gun mounting,
but at least the 75 mm gun was able to
destroy German tanks invulnerable to the
old 2-pounders.

Sherman

Specification
Crew: 5
Engine power: 400 bhp (298.4 kW)
Combat weight: 66,502 lb (30.160 kg)
Max speed: 23.6 mph (38 km/h)
Length: 19.16 ft (5.84 m)
Range: 99.36 miles (160 km)
Width: 8.79 ft (2.68 m)
Main gun: 2.96 in (75 mm)
Height: 9.74 ft (2.97 m)
Armour: 0.98—2.01 in (25—51 mm)

The Sherman was the name given by the British
to the American-made Medium Tank M4. It was
based on the hull of the M3 (the Grant). The M4
had the same engine and suspension as the M3,
but the M3's side doors were omitted. Engine
supply in the production of the M4 was a
problem because the intended Wright Continental
was also needed for aircraft. Several other
engines were used, the Chrysler Multibank engine
of the M4A4 (which was in fact five car engines
driving a common main shaft) was so big that
the hull of the tank had to be lengthened.

Churchill Mark IV

Specification
Crew: 5
Engine power: 350 bhp (261.1 kW)
Combat weight: 98,611 lb (40,640 kg)
Max speed: 12.42 mph (20 km/h)
Length: 24.74 ft (7.54 m)
Range: 217.35 miles (350 km)
Width: 8.99 ft (2.74 m)
Main gun: 2.96 in (75 mm)
Height: 10.99 ft (3.35 m)
Armour: 0.98–6 in (25–152 mm)

The Churchill Mark IV NA75 was a sub-mark of
the Mark IX and the Mark XI. It was specific
to the North Africa campaign and was created
by rearming Churchill Mark IXs and Mark XIs
with 75 mm guns taken from wrecked Shermans.
Because of their weight and stability,
Churchills were also adapted into 'special
role' tanks, in order to carry heavy
equipment, such as bridges. In addition, the
Churchill AVRE was armed with a mortar which
launched a heavy demolition charge.

Panzer III

Specification (Ausf F)
Crew: 5
Engine power: 300 bhp
Combat weight: 43,659 lb (19,800 kg)
Max speed: 24.84 mph (40 km/h)
Length: 17.65 ft (5.38 m)
Range: 102.47 miles (165 km)
Width: 9.55 ft (2.91 m)
Main gun: 1.46 in (37 mm)
Height: 8.01 ft (2.44 m)
Armour: 0.47—1.18 in (12—30 mm)

The German-manufactured Panzer III was a
development of the Panzer I and Panzer II
tanks. The Panzer III was designed with a
turret-mounted 1.46 in (3.7 cm) gun and two
machine-guns. A heavier gun could also be
mounted if required. It had a crew of five:
commander, driver, gunner, loader and radio
operator. The main problem for the German
forces with the Panzer III was that
production was so slow that there were never
enough. As a result many Panzer divisions in
the early years of the war were filled out
with Czech tanks.

Panzer IV

Specification (Ausf H)
Crew: 5
Engine power: 300 bhp
Combat weight: 55,125 lb (25,000 kg)
Max speed: 23.60 mph (38 km/h)
Length: 23.03 ft (7.02 m)
Range: 130.41 miles (210 km)
Width: 9.45 ft (2.88 m)
Main gun: 2.96 in (75 mm)
Height: 8.79 ft (2.68 m)
Armour: 0.32—3.15 in (8—80 mm)

The Panzer IV became the workhorse of the
Panzer divisions. Originally intended as a
heavy support for the Panzer III units, the
Panzer IV had a short 2.96 in (7.5 cm)
main gun and a five-man crew, all provided
with an intercom system, an innovation at
that time. The Panzer IV also provided the
basis for many other combat vehicles. For
example, self-propelled guns and air-
defence tanks were all mounted on a Panzer
IV chassis.

Carro Armato M13/40

Specification
Crew: 4
Engine power: 105 bhp (78.33 kW)
Combat weight: 30,879 lb (14,000 kg)
Max speed: 19.75 mph (31.8 km/h)
Length: 16.13 ft (4.915 m)
Range: 124.2 miles (200 km)
Width: 7.22 ft (2.2 m)
Main gun: 1.85 in (47 mm)
Height: 7.78 ft (2.37 m)
Armour: 0.55—1.58 in (14—40 mm)

The Carro Armato M13/40 was the main Italian
tank used in the Desert War, a development from
the earlier M11/39. The M13/40's 47 mm anti-
tank gun was an excellent weapon, accurate and
able to penetrate the armour of many British
tanks beyond the effective range of their
2-pounder weapons. During the Desert War, the
Australians and the British often used captured
Carro Armato M13/40 tanks; in fact, at one time
the British had over 100 in use.

25-Pounder

Specification
Crew: 6
Calibre: 87.6 mm
Weight: 1 ton 1730 lb (1,800 kg)
Barrel length: 10 ft 6 in (2.35 m)
Elevation: -5°/+ 40°

The 25-pounder was one of the classic field
pieces of artillery of the Second World War.
It entered service at the start of the war and
made its mark during the opening barrage at
Alamein in 1942. It was used in all the
theatres of the war, from the desert to
jungle. Its comparative light weight and ease
of use stood it in good stead, even when it
was out-ranged by the enemy.

Chapter 7
Outnumbered

New orders from Captain Mason in Tank 333 came through within the next few minutes.

'We're going to set up an ambush for the enemy. All tanks to withdraw to new positions half a mile back from the ridge, in two groups of four, leaving a gap half a mile wide between them to allow the German tanks to come through. The group on the west of the ridge will be led by Tank 333, the group to the east by Tank 247. The tank at the rear of the west group is to keep its main gun aimed at the first German tank through the gap, the tank at the rear of the east group to keep the second tank in its sights, and so on down the line. Fire on my mark. All lights to be kept extinguished throughout this manoeuvre, at least until the order is given to fire.'

I turned Bessie round and our east group

drove out in a spread-out line until we had reached the designated point half a mile from the ridge. Then we turned so that our guns were pointing towards the gap in the ridge, but clear of hitting the west group.

We took up our positions with just two minutes to go before the German tanks were due to appear.

'Engines off,' came the orders.

I switched off the engine. Harry slid a shell into the breech of the main gun. Chalky checked the rounds about to be fed in the machine-gun. I turned to Chalky and gave him a grin.

'Don't worry,' I whispered. 'This tank is the best there is. And, like I said, Weston is a good commander. We'll be OK.'

We waited. We could hear the engines and the tracks of the Panzers clearly now. Our hope was that they would roll straight past us, at least long enough for us to gain the element of surprise. But we'd have to have a lot of luck on our side, the sky was already starting to show streaks of light. Dawn wasn't far away.

The first of the Panzers drove through the gap in the ridge. We let it continue. There was a pause, then came the second, then the third. They were assuming that if they were to be attacked it would have happened at once, as soon as the first of their tanks appeared. Mason was counting on lulling them into a sense of security, letting as many as possible get through, and then hitting them from behind.

Unfortunately for us, the commander of the sixth Panzer tank was more watchful than his comrades. He obviously spotted one of the tanks in the west group because even from the distance we were, I saw the tank turret start to swing and knew that he was getting ready to fire. Captain Mason had seen it too, because the radio crackled, and then Prof shouted the order: 'Fire!'

All of our tanks opened up at once, their shells hammering into the target tanks they'd been allocated, and the night sky was suddenly filled with fire as the shells struck home, into the Panzers.

Even as our first target burst into flames, Weston had ordered George to aim the gun at the next Panzer just coming through the gap in the ridge. George fired at the same time as one of our other tanks, who obviously had the same idea. The Panzer in the gap blew up, and then sank down on to the sand, broken, with black smoke and orange flames pouring out from its shattered turret.

Seven of their tanks were now out of action, and the gap in the ridge was blocked.

'Turn to guard against the sides of the ridge!' came the order.

All our tanks swung round so that our guns were now pointed at the far ends of the ridge, the only way left for the remaining Panzers to attack us. Some of the Panzers had already begun firing blind over the ridge, but their shells flew harmlessly over our heads.

Panzer tanks began to appear at the far end of the ridge, about a mile away, their great guns swivelling towards us.

'Target and fire at will!' commanded Weston.

Over my headphones I could hear Harry grunting with the effort as he lifted the heavy shells and loaded, while George fired. WHOOMP WHOOMP WHOOMP, one shell after the other. The first Panzer sank down as George's shell struck, crippling it. The gun of the second Panzer was already swinging round towards us and I tensed, waiting to be hit, but the shell missed and crashed into the tank next to us.

'See what you can do, driver,' came Weston's voice over my headphones.

'Will do, skipper,' I said.

I began to move Bessie forwards, weaving to the left and right all the time to avoid the Panzers getting an easy bearing on us. Fortunately, with the Grant's gyro-stabilizers, Harry and George still had control of aiming the gun, despite the movement.

Some of the Panzers were now actually coming over the top of the ridge, bearing down on us, guns blazing. There was a lot of noise coming from the radio now as messages flew back and forth between Command Tank 333 and the other tanks, but Prof wasn't bothering to relay any of them unless they had a direct bearing on our position and course of action. Every now and then we heard an explosion near to us, and realized that one of our own tanks had taken a hit. Through the window of my hatch I saw one of our tanks break away and begin to make a run for it, followed by another, heading back to our own lines. Neither made it. As I watched both of them took direct hits right into the back, exploding the petrol tank and pushing the engine right through into the hull. Both tanks blew up. The poor devils inside wouldn't have had a chance.

'Charge towards the enemy!' ordered Weston.

I swung Bessie towards the top of the ridge, and charged. It may have sounded a crazy thing to do, rush at the enemy, but it was a sensible decision. For one thing the most vulnerable part of a tank is the rear, where the engine and petrol tank are. For another, if you rush at an enemy, firing all the time, you hope it puts them off taking proper aim at you.

I drove on, and now beside me Chalky was firing the machine-gun at the tank we were approaching. Some of the bullets bounced off the Panzer's armour plating, but some must have penetrated the vision hatch because the German tank suddenly veered wildly to one side and crashed into another Panzer.

George and Harry were still keeping up the firing, only now they'd switched to the smaller gun, the 37 mm. At this closer range it was just as effective and faster to load and fire.

It all sounds as if we were organized, but the truth is that the battle was chaotic. When this much metal is flying around at enormous speeds and you can be killed from one second to another, you just do what you can to survive: dodging, weaving, and firing back, and doing your best to keep a clear head. But you can have the clearest head in the world and it won't do you a bit of good if the enemy hits you with a lucky or a well-aimed shot.

The noise, as in all tank battles, was deafening. We had now given up trying to hear any instructions, even over the headphones. We couldn't hear a thing except the crash of guns and the sounds of explosions. Bessie rocked a couple of times as stray German shells hit us, but our armour held and the shells just bounced off to explode outside the tank.

I don't know how long we had been fighting, it seemed like hours, but I'd heard it always does, even if it's just minutes. I kept Bessie rolling backwards and forwards along the cover of the ridge while George and Harry fired their 37 mm and Chalky let fly with the machine-gun. The only one of our tanks that I could see still moving was Captain Mason's 333. It wasn't too far from us, just about fifty yards away. Even as I watched it took a couple of hits. Its metal caterpillar tracks slid off like an orange being peeled and its turret buckled. Another German shell thudded into it, and the tank flipped half over. The figure of Captain Mason fell out of the hatch, dropping like a rag doll to the sand, where he lay rolling in agony. A Panzer was heading straight for him, and at the speed it was going it didn't look like it was going to stop. Mason was about to be crushed beneath its tracks.

Then Weston did one of the bravest things I've ever seen. He shouted 'Cover me!', flipped open the hatch, clambered out of the turret and dropped down on to the sand. Then he ran towards the wounded Mason in an attempt to drag him out of the path of the oncoming Panzer. Harry and George both grabbed at the Browning machine-guns. They and Chalky opened fire at the Panzer, shooting over the crouching Weston's head, their tracers of bullets smashing into the hull and the tank's turret. I drove Bessie forwards to where Mason lay, ready to pick him and Weston up. The Panzer still powered on, its huge mass towering over Mason's fallen body.

Weston got there in time. He grabbed Mason under the arms and hauled him to one side, just as the Panzer rolled past, right over the spot where Mason had been lying. I don't know why the Panzer gun crew didn't hit us with their main gun. Maybe they had problems with it. Maybe it had jammed. That happens with some guns after they've been firing non-stop. Whatever the reason, if they had opened fire they would have blasted us into nothing. As it was, George suddenly let fly with the 37 mm and hit them smack in the front, right in the driver's hatch.

I was trying to keep my eye on Weston and Mason down there on the sand, and positioning Bessie between them and the other Panzers.

Suddenly I saw Weston put his hands up. It was then I realized how quiet it was all of a sudden. All the tanks had stopped firing.

'They've got him,' said Chalky beside me, shock and anger in his voice.

A machine-gun was trained on the lonely figure of Weston. Then another. In the silence a voice called out to us in broken English across the desert night.

'Yours is the only tank left, Britishers. You cannot win now. Surrender, or we will shoot your comrade. And then we will shoot you.'

'What shall we do?' asked Prof's voice in my headphones. He was talking to all of us, not just to me.

I looked out through the window of my hatch. We were surrounded by Panzers, all with their main guns pointed straight at us. If we resisted we'd be blasted into a mass of crumpled metal.

'You have ten seconds!' called the voice. 'After that, I give the orders to fire and you will all die. Ten. Nine. Eight . . .'

As we listened to the German commander count down, Harry said grimly: 'We haven't got a chance. At least if we give up now, maybe we can save ourselves later.'

The German commander counted on.

'. . . Six. Five. Four . . .'

'Maybe if we started firing first we'd catch them by surprise?' suggested Chalky, desperation in his voice.

'And two seconds later Weston would be dead on the sand, and we'd be turned into ashes,' Prof said. He sighed. 'Outnumbered like we are, I don't think we've got much choice, lads.'

'. . . Two. One.'

I heard the turret hatch scrape back, then George's voice shouted out: 'All right! We're coming out!'

Chalky and I hauled ourselves up and out of the driver's compartment and joined

George, Harry, Prof and Weston on the sand, our hands held up over our heads. Some of the Germans came out of their tanks now and joined us on the sand, their guns trained on us. One look at the grim expressions on their faces was enough to tell us they'd shoot us if we tried anything.

I looked around at the scene. It was carnage, smoke from burning tanks drifting around us, bodies scattered about on the sand. Captain Mason still lay just a few feet away from us. It was pretty obvious to all of us that he was already dead. Weston looked down at him and shrugged.

'Still at least I saved him from being run over,' Weston said.

'Silence!' snapped a voice, then a German officer stepped past the soldiers with their machine-guns and glared at us.

'As commanding officer of this unit, I insist that we are treated as prisoners of war in accordance with regulations,' demanded Weston.

'You do not need to insist,' the German officer replied coldly. 'The army of the Third Reich does everything by the rule book.'

'Only checking,' said Weston. 'In that case, take us to your leader!'

The way Weston said it, trying to make a joke despite the mess we were in, and all the death around us, made the rest of us want to laugh. Well, it made me, George and Harry want to laugh. Chalky and Prof both looked nervous about the whole thing.

The Germans searched us for weapons. Then they made us sit down cross-legged on the sand with our hands on our heads.

'As soon as the transport arrives you will be taken to the nearest transit camp,' said the officer. 'You are now prisoners of war. For all of you, the war is over.'

Chapter 8
Captured

As the sun came up on a new day, two armoured cars loaded with armed German soldiers, and an open truck, arrived. When they pulled up near us we had been sitting on the sand with our hands on our heads for nearly two hours. In those hours we'd had plenty of time to take in the aftermath of last night's battle. Bessie was the only tank of our original eight that had survived. The other seven had been destroyed. As far as we could see we'd taken out almost twenty of the Panzers, which was a pretty good rate of exchange in war terms for our side, but in human terms it was a catastrophe. All those men dead.

I sat there, hands on my head, and looked at Bessie. Her hatch hung open. Her sides were scorched and scarred from shell bursts, her tracks damaged. But she'd done us proud. Her armour had resisted all that the Panzers had thrown at us, her steering had got us out of trouble during the battle, her stabilizers had kept our guns firing firmly and steadily throughout. She was a great tank. And now we were losing her.

The tank commander handed us over to another German officer. He and his men tied our wrists with strong cord, then they loaded us at gunpoint on to the open truck. That done, they tied our legs together so that we couldn't jump off the truck and run away while it was moving. Three of the armed soldiers jumped into the back with us and kept their guns on us. We lay roped together and just glared at them. There wasn't a lot to say.

The lead armoured car started up and we set off in convoy, one car at the front, us in the truck and the second car keeping watch on us from behind.

By now the early sun was starting to get hot. The desert around us looked smooth as we travelled, leaving the scene of the battle behind us. The wreckage of twisted metal. Birds circling overhead, waiting to get their pickings from the dead. Apart from the sounds of those birds, it was quiet. The quiet of the dawn after the battle of the night before.

We drove across the desert for an hour or so, about twenty miles I guessed from the speed of the convoy over that terrain. From that, and the position of the sun, we knew that we were now well behind Axis lines.

Then we saw a camp ahead: lines of tents and vehicles, mainly lorries and jeeps. Next to this camp was a large compound surrounded by a very high wire fence. There were men inside. As we got nearer we saw that they were Allied soldiers, about a hundred of them. It was a prisoner-of-war transit camp.

'Once we get behind that wire it'll be even harder to get out,' grumbled George.

'Are you suggesting we make a break for it?' whispered Harry.

I took a quick look at the intent faces of the armed soldiers guarding us.

'I don't think that's a good idea,' I muttered. 'Tied together like this, we wouldn't get five yards before we'd all be dead. At least while we're alive we've got a chance.'

'Silence!' shouted one of the soldiers.

We shut up. It only took another five minutes or so before our convoy pulled up in

front of the first tent in the camp. The
soldiers undid the ropes from our ankles and
wrists and pushed us roughly down from
the back of the truck on to the sand. Once
more, we lined up. The German officer in
charge got down from his jeep and went up to
Weston.

'It is now my duty to hand you over to the
Italian army,' he announced.

We shot quick looks at each other. This
was bad news. We'd all heard reports from
prisoners who'd escaped about how they
were treated in the different prisoner-of-war
camps, and the Italians were known to treat
Allied prisoners badly. Whether it was
revenge for the humiliation they had experi-
enced back in 1941, when Wavell's 30,000
men had taken the whole Italian army
prisoner, all 250,000 of them, we didn't
know. All we did have were reports of Italian
guards beating and shooting unarmed
prisoners, and sometimes leaving the
wounded to suffer.

Weston caught our looks of concern. He
obviously felt just as worried about our
future as prisoners.

'I must remind you, as an officer, that we
were taken prisoner by an officer of the

German army, and as such we should remain prisoners of the German army.'

'And I must tell you that we of the German army are here to fight a war, not to look after prisoners!' the officer snapped back.

By now we had been joined by a patrol of Italian soldiers, led by an officer who had more medals on his tunic than anyone I'd ever seen before, short of a general.

The enemy officers gave each other a salute before talking briefly in German.

A short time later we were marched into the compound under a guard of Italian soldiers. The main gates of the compound clanged shut behind us, then they were locked and chained. We were now properly prisoners of war.

It didn't take us long to get settled in. A prisoner-of-war camp is run much the same as any other army camp. The most senior officer is in charge of the Camp Committee, consisting of the other officers. They give the orders out to the rest of the prisoners. They also deal with the enemy commanders on behalf of the prisoners. In the case of this particular camp, the most senior officer was a Major Benson. There were two captains and four lieutenants, including Weston. Weston's rank automatically put him on the Camp Committee.

These camps weren't actually proper prisoner-of-war camps: they were called transit camps, places to keep the prisoners until they could be moved on. Our transit camp was just a large square, flat, open area of hard and rocky sand with a tall double fence going all the way round it. There were no tents, no cover of any kind, except what the men had been able to make themselves out of their great-coats, those that had them. Groups of men sat around, talking or playing makeshift games. The mood of everyone was one of boredom and frustration. There was no privacy.

The Italians had set up machine-gun posts at each corner of the compound, the guns aimed in at us. Any trouble and they could fire in through the fence and mow us down.

While Weston went to introduce himself to Major Benson, we sat down on the hot sand with a group of prisoners.

They were a mixed bunch, just like the rest of the army – English, Scots, Welsh, Irish, Australians, New Zealanders, Rhodesians, South Africans, Indians. We soon learnt how the prisoner-of-war routine worked.

'They take us in batches over to Italy,' said Dirk, a South African private. 'Once they've got enough, they load us into trucks and then take us to the nearest port.'

'How many's enough?' I asked.

Dirk shrugged. 'A few hundred. It depends. To be honest you never know where you are with these Italians. They're all a bit chaotic. One week they may take four lorry-loads. The next, just one lorry-load. I suppose it depends on how many they're taking from the other transit camps.'

'How long have you been at this place?' asked Prof.

'Two weeks,' said Dirk. 'My guess is I'll be going on the next load. It wouldn't surprise me to find they clear us all out in one go.'

The big complaint among most of the men seemed to be the lack of cover. In the daytime the sun blazed down, and at night it was cold, as is often the way in the desert. Those who had been captured with their great-coats were the lucky ones; they had something to wrap round at night to keep warm. Some of the others had dug themselves holes in the sand to keep warm at night, though they said you didn't want to dig too deep because the further down you went, the colder the sand was. Make a bed-shelter from the top layer of sand, that's what they advised. The sun heated it up during the day and it would keep you warm for a few hours at night, at least.

The whole business of being exposed like this, the very fact of having been taken prisoner and now being herded into this compound like sheep, meant morale was very low. Most of the blokes seemed to have given up on the war and many were looking forward to being shipped over to Italy to a proper prisoner-of-war camp.

I saw Weston heading back towards us, having just finished his meeting with Major Benson. I signalled to the rest of our crew and we joined him over by the fence, a bit apart from the rest of the prisoners. He told us much the same story as Dirk had. The Italians were waiting for more lorries to arrive to take us all to the nearest port, and then on to Italy, where we'd spend the rest of the war in a camp.

'Not for me!' grunted George.

'Nor me!' I said.

Harry, Prof and Chalky nodded. We all looked at Weston.

He nodded in agreement: 'We're getting out,' he whispered.

Chapter 9
Prisoners of War

We spent the rest of the day walking around the inside of the compound, circuit after circuit, in pairs. Me and Weston. George and Harry. Prof and Chalky. The Italian guards thought we were exercising and laughed at us. In reality we were checking every part of the wire fence, looking for the weak spot. We didn't find it.

In the afternoon the compound gates opened and armed Italian soldiers ordered us back, while others brought in three long wooden trestle tables. The prisoners detailed by the Camp Committee then came forwards and set the trestle tables up. That done, the Italians brought in two large steaming tureens. As the smell of food hit me, I realized I hadn't eaten for nearly a whole day and my stomach was desperate for food.

We lined up at the tables. Each of us picked up a metal plate and a spoon, then one by one we filed past to have our plates filled up with a kind of stew. Tinned meat with some sort of pasta, by the look of it. Plus a bit of hard bread. I was so hungry I didn't care what it was.

We found ourselves a separate place on the sand, sat down and began to eat. While we ate, we talked.

'Right,' said Weston, 'let's have some reports. The fence?'

We all shook our heads.

'The first problem is it's a double fence,' said Prof. 'Even if we get through the first fence, we've still got to get through the second one. And by that time the chances are the guards will have spotted us. They're not that brilliant, but they don't have to be brilliant to guard us out here in the middle of the desert.'

'We can't get over the fence for the same reason,' added George. 'Plus, as soon as we get on the top we'd present the perfect target.'

'And tunnelling under's out as well,' sighed Chalky. 'If we tried to do it quickly, we'd be spotted.'

'And we don't have time to tunnel out slowly because the lorries could be here any day and take us all away,' nodded Weston. He didn't seem at all disturbed by what we'd just said. He'd obviously been expecting it. He looked around at us. 'Any disagreements on all those points so far?'

We all munched our bread and shook our heads.

'Then we're all agreed that we can't get out through, over or under the fence,' he said. 'Which leaves only one way out.'

'Fly?' suggested George.

We all laughed. Then I suggested: 'We wait till they come to get us in the lorries.'

Weston nodded.

'My thought exactly,' he said. 'From what everyone's said they'll be coming pretty soon, and when they do they'll take all of us. After all, there are only about a hundred of us here.'

'We can't do it on our own, skipper,' said Harry. 'What about the rest of the blokes? We'll have to let them know.'

'I know,' agreed Weston. 'I'll talk to the major and put it to the Camp Committee.'

'A mass break-out,' mused Prof.

'What do we do if the Camp Committee doesn't agree?' I asked.

'There's only one thing we can do,' said

Weston. 'We escape on our own, without the others. Agreed?'

We looked at each other and nodded.

'Agreed,' we said together.

Chapter 10
Planning the Escape

Next morning after breakfast – if you could call the watery gruel that we were given 'breakfast' – I went for a stroll around the inner fence with Prof, and we had a surprise. There, parked about a hundred yards outside the fence, in between the lorries and jeeps, was Bessie. The Germans had brought her in and the Italians were keeping her on display like a prize trophy, just to let us know they were winning this desert war.

As we looked at her, an idea struck me.

'We could use Bessie to escape,' I whispered to Prof.

Prof glanced at me in surprise, then at Bessie, then back at me again. Behind his glasses his eyes looked at me as if I'd gone mad with the sun.

'Think about it,' I said. 'It'd be perfect.'

And I explained my thinking to him, very briefly, in a low voice. I didn't want anyone overhearing. It only took a few minutes of talking to him, and then Prof was nodding in agreement.

'It *could* work,' he said thoughtfully.

'Of course it could!' I said. 'Let's go and see the others before Weston goes before the Camp Committee.'

We hurried back to where George, Harry and Chalky were making a set of playing cards out of old Italian newspapers. Weston was just on his way to see the major to put our escape idea to him. I made sure we couldn't be overheard before telling them all that we'd seen Bessie and my idea for using her to escape.

'Escape in a tank?' asked Harry. 'Are you potty? At the speed that moves a man on a bike will be able to catch us!'

'Not with Bessie!' I replied. 'Twenty-six miles an hour, top speed. She's a good tank! Plus we'll be armed. Machine-guns. The main gun. Get to our tank and we can blast this camp, stopping the Italians radioing for help. Shoot up their vehicles. It will give us all the time we need to get back to our own lines.'

'Providing the Germans have left the ammunition in the tank,' said George.

'They're bound to have!' I said. 'After all, they'll want to use it themselves. I bet it's only here because it's in reserve. They'll paint out our symbol and put their own on it. Anyway, I don't want to leave Bessie behind when we go. She's too good a tank to abandon like that.'

'If you think about it from the communication side, it's a good idea,' added Prof. 'We'll have a radio. Once we get back within radio range we could contact HQ and let them know what's going on.'

'Providing we don't get blown up before that,' grunted Harry, still not convinced. 'I reckon we'd be better off with something faster. One of those Italian lorries. Or a jeep with a machine-gun on it.'

'And getting shot at by our own side,' laughed Weston. 'Yes, I think John's idea is a good one. We get out, get Bessie back, and off we go. All I have to do is sell the idea to the others.'

While Weston went off to talk to the Camp Committee, I took a walk to the wire fence to look at Bessie again. An Italian soldier arrived beside her carrying a tin of paint and a brush. As I suspected, he was going to paint out our British army symbols, and then re-paint her with Italian colours. He didn't look like he was very keen on the job, but then most soldiers aren't keen on doing those sort of jobs. A soldier in the army can make paint-ing anything last weeks, because he knows that once he's finished one painting job he'll just be given another, so why hurry and make more work for yourself?

The Italian soldier began painting over our symbols with very slow and careful brush strokes, taking his time. It pained me to see our symbols being painted out like this, but I knew in my heart that we'd be getting Bessie back soon, and it didn't matter what colours she wore: she was *our* tank.

The Camp Committee of seven officers were in deep discussion in the centre of the com-pound. You may think it odd that this sort of thing could go on: officers discussing some-thing like an escape right in plain view of everyone, but in a way that was why they could do it. Because there was no cover and everyone just sat or walked around looking listless and defeated, the guards didn't think that anyone would try anything. No one had tried to escape yet. The fences were too high.

The machine-guns kept everyone in their place, and quiet. The transit camp was a long way away from the actual fighting. All this made the guards just that little bit too complacent, which was good for our escape plan. If the Camp Committee agreed to it.

I turned and saw that Weston wasn't having an easy time of it. There were arguments going on among the officers, though no one was raising their voice. Every now and then Major Benson lifted a hand to quieten someone down, then the discussion resumed.

The Italian guards watched all this from their machine-gun posts with amusement. As far as they were concerned the Camp Committee was discussing things like the quality of the food or the lack of shelter. That was what they usually talked about, and then the major would take their complaints to the camp commander. The guards weren't bothered; they were quite happy for the prisoners to squabble among themselves. Divided and unhappy prisoners were less likely to get together and cause them problems.

Finally the Camp Committee finished its session. The officers went back to their units to report. I left the fence and hurried towards our crew as Weston returned, trying to walk as casually as possible so as not to alert the guards that anything special was going on. I looked at the faces of the other officers as I walked. Some of them looked pleased, but at least two looked very unhappy. I arrived back with Harry, George, Prof and Chalky just as Weston did.

'We're go!' announced Weston triumphantly.

'All of them?' asked Harry. Like me, he'd seen the expression on the faces of those two officers.

'Most,' said Weston. 'The other two will back it. After all, we're in the army and orders are orders.'

Talking in low tones, he outlined the plan. As Weston spoke to us, the other officers were doing the same, spreading the word around.

'When the lorries arrive to take us away, we line up and go along with it, doing nothing to put the Italians on their guard. There will be about ten Italians in charge of loading us, all armed. Once we start to get on to the lorries, two men will begin an argument, with one accusing the other of pushing him.'

'Which two?' asked George.

'Two of the Australians,' said Weston. 'Captain Fraser of the Ninth Australian

Infantry Division reckons two of his men will be delighted to do it. Their argument will turn into a fight. The guards will come over to break it up, but the fight will spread, with other soldiers joining in. For a few seconds there will be chaos, and in those few moments all the action will have to take place. The men nearest to the guards will jump them, bringing them down and taking their guns off them. Once they've got the guns they open fire on the other Italians. It will all have to be done very, very fast, before the Italians realize what's happening. We have force of numbers on our side, but they've got the weapons. During all this we take one of the guns and make for our tank. It's our job to recapture Bessie, start her up, and then cause havoc while the rest of them get back on to the lorries and make their escape. Once the lorries are on their way, we can leave. It was on that basis that I sold it to them. Everyone else goes first, we go last and give them cover with Bessie.'

'Why were there some grim faces among the officers?' asked Harry.

'Because they know that it's not going to be that simple,' said Weston. 'The Italians will start shooting and men are going to get killed.

Some of them are very close to being taken to safety after two years of hard fighting, even if it is only to a prisoner-of-war camp, and they're not happy about taking the risk of being killed.'

'You mean they'd rather stay as prisoners than take the chance of getting back to their own units?' said Chalky, amazed.

'Don't blame them so quickly,' replied Weston. 'When you've been out here as long as some of us, and seen some of the fighting and death that we've seen, maybe you'd be just as keen for a rest.'

'Has anyone any idea when the next lot of lorries are due to take us away?' I asked.

'No,' said Weston. 'It could be any day now. It could be weeks. All we can do . . . is wait.'

Chapter 11
Break-out!

And so we waited. The days passed. We spent them sitting around, talking, playing games of cards with the makeshift pack that George, Harry and Chalky had made. Sometimes we played noughts and crosses in the sand. We ate twice a day beneath the hot sun: watery gruel for breakfast and a hot kind of stew in the afternoon, with hard bread. It was the same routine every day. None of the prisoners did anything to upset this routine, so the guards were kept happy. The whole atmosphere was relaxed and easy, which was exactly what we wanted it to be. We wanted the guards to feel safe and secure. That way we hoped they'd be at ease when the time came for us to get on the lorries, so they would be taken by surprise when the trouble started.

We spent four days like this, just lazing around in the heat during the day, and shivering in the cold of the desert night, trying to sleep. On the fifth day we knew that something was up. There was a new tension about the guards. They started preparing three of the lorries that were parked up, and rushing around, with lots of shouting of orders. We all kept quiet, watching the goings-on through the wire fence. In the distance we could see a large dust cloud getting nearer. More lorries were on their way.

Armed soldiers appeared, who took guard at the compound entrance. The gates were opened and an Italian officer came in. His second in command stood next to him and began to shout in English.

'Attention! For you the war is over. You are very lucky. You are about to go somewhere safe. Gather all your belongings and line up.'

Major Benson then took over, stepping forward and issuing exactly the same orders to line up, but without telling us how lucky we were.

We took up our possessions, what few we had, and started to form a line by the gates.

Weston made sure that he, George, Harry, Chalky and Prof were near the back of the line. I had volunteered to be the one to use the gun to help Crew 247 get to Bessie, so I positioned myself further along the line near to the two Australians who had volunteered to stage the fight. That way I would be near enough to step in and get the gun. The Australians were both big men, with big arms and tough-looking faces.

We stood at ease under the watchful eyes of the armed Italian soldiers, and waited. The lorries were getting nearer and nearer now. We all kept quiet, giving the appearance of complete listlessness. We didn't want to alert the Italians that anything might go wrong with their operation. So far there had been ten or twelve transports of prisoners from this camp, with no problems. There was no reason for them to think that this one might be different.

The three lorries from the base had been moved to just outside the gates. Four new lorries arrived. Three of them went and parked up, and the fourth joined the other waiting lorries. That made sense: they couldn't transport prisoners until they had replacement lorries, otherwise the transit camp would be left without vehicles.

The armed guards now moved into the

compound and began shouting at us in Italian. Although we couldn't understand what they were saying, the way they gestured with their guns at us, at the gate and at the waiting lorries made their message clear enough.

We shuffled forwards, heads down, shoulders slumped, out through the compound's open gates, heading for the waiting lorries. The guards had relaxed again, sensing there would be no trouble from us.

Twenty-five men clambered on board the first lorry and the guards relaxed just a little bit more.

The next batch of men were just starting to haul themselves up on the tailboard of the second lorry when it started. One of the Australians pushed the other out of the way, as if to get on the lorry before him. The other Australian didn't say a word, but just belted him. It was supposed to be a fake punch, but it looked real enough to me. The one who'd been hit crashed down to the ground and his attacker jumped on him. Soon the pair were rolling about in the sand, punching, grabbing, shouting and swearing. Two of the nearest guards ran over to them with their guns raised, while another couple kept the other prisoners back. Rifle butts crashed down on the arms of the fighting prisoners. Suddenly the two Australians leapt up from the ground and grabbed the guns, pulling the two guards down. Caught off balance, the Italians fell over. The other guards heard them yell out in alarm and instinctively turned to see what was going on. That was the moment everyone had been waiting for. We bundled forwards, jumping on the other guards, who shouted for help.

The remaining guards saw what was happening and started firing their weapons, but they had to shoot over the heads of the prisoners in case they hit their own men.

The fallen guards were desperately trying to hang on to their rifles, but as the punches and kicks rained down on them they had no chance. One of them had a machine-gun. He let go of it to try and protect himself. I managed to snatch it up from the ground. I fired a burst into the air to let Weston and the others know that I was armed.

'Go!' Weston yelled at our crew, and we all began running towards Bessie, me keeping well to the right of Weston, Prof, Harry, George and Chalky so that I didn't get them in my line of fire.

Behind me the prisoners with the other three guards' guns opened fire. As the Italian's dropped to the sand, more prisoners rushed forwards to grab the fallen guards' weapons. The Italians were now in terrible confusion. Some of the prisoners had dragged the drivers of the lorries out of their cabs.

As we were running towards Bessie, some Italian soldiers appeared out of their tents, guns at the ready. I let off a burst at them, hitting one in the legs, while Chalky scrambled into Bessie's co-driver's seat. He started up the Browning machine-gun, maintaining constant fire, shooting a stream of bullets across the Italians' position to hold them down and keep them from returning fire.

The rest of the crew took this opportunity to climb up on to the hull, and into the turret. Once they were all inside the tank, I ran for the driver's compartment, firing as I went. George opened up with his machine-gun, and he and Chalky hammered bullets into the Italians' tents and vehicles as I jumped up on to Bessie's hull and dropped down into my driver's seat.

About a hundred yards away the lorries were now full with prisoners and were being driven off.

In between machine-gun bursts we could hear shouting in Italian as an officer tried to restore some sort of order to the situation.

I pulled on my headphones and throat mike set and heard Weston order: 'Right. Let's get this thing started up.'

It was then I discovered that we were out of petrol.

Chapter 12

No Way Out

'Sorry, sir,' I reported. 'No fuel.'

Through my headphones I heard George swear. Then he said, 'I'll get some. I know where they keep their fuel supply. I've had nothing better to do for days but work out the lie of this rotten camp.'

'How far is it?' asked Weston.

'About a hundred yards away, over by those parked-up lorries. If you can cover me and keep them down I should be all right.'

'We'll cover you,' said Weston. 'Right, men. Hit them with the machine-guns, one gun at a time, Atkins first, then White, for five-second bursts, and keep firing alternately in that order. Fire.'

Harry opened fire for his five-second burst, then he stopped. Chalky took over, then Harry carried on, and so on. Meanwhile we heard the metal clonk of the hatch flipping back as George clambered out. He slid down the turret and jumped down to the sand. Soon I saw him out of my hatch window, dodging and zigzagging, running for the lorries. I saw the ground behind him start to flick up as bullets thudded into it, just missing him. Then George threw himself at the lorries and rolled into cover.

'He's going to have a difficult time getting back, sir,' I told Weston. 'There's an open patch of ground which they've got their sights on. They nearly got him first time. When he returns he'll be carrying two heavy cans of petrol. He'll be an easy target.'

'Where's their shooting coming from?' asked Weston.

'Hard to tell, sir,' I said. 'We've got most of them pinned down so they can't fire directly at us, but I reckon there's someone in that tent to our left. They're right next to the fuel dump and they've got a clean line of fire to just in front of the lorries.'

'Can you hit that tent, Atkins? White?' asked Weston.

'Only the top of it, sir,' said Harry. 'I can't hit it low, which is where their rifles will be.'

'Same problem for me, sir,' added Chalky.

111

'Those armoured cars are in the way. If the Italians are lying down on the ground, they're safe.'

'We have to do something, sir,' I said. 'George won't make it back across that open stretch.'

'And if he doesn't, we're stuck here,' muttered Harry.

'Maybe we could hit the tent with our main gun, sir,' suggested Prof.

'Not a good idea, Read,' commented Weston. 'At this close range we'd likely blow up their fuel dump and Gunner Hoskins with it. No, someone's going to have to get closer and deal with the problem.'

'I'll do it, sir,' I volunteered.

'I will, sir,' added Harry.

'Smith volunteered first. He goes,' said Weston.

'Begging your pardon, sir,' put in Harry, 'but Smith is our driver. If anything should go wrong, we're going to need him to get this tank back to our own lines.'

'Begging your pardon, sir,' I said, 'but White is our co-driver. He could take Bessie back.'

'Let's hope it doesn't come to that,' said Weston. 'Atkins, White, begin covering fire on my mark. Ready, Smith?'

I hefted the machine-gun in my hands.

'Ready, sir,' I said.

'Right,' said Weston. 'Fire!'

Chalky and Harry began firing. Quickly, I climbed up from the driver's seat and got out of the front compartment. I slid down the hull to the sand and began firing at the Italian positions. The shooting that was keeping George from getting back was coming from a tent hidden behind a couple of lorries. I ran to the lorries and dropped to the ground, then crawled under the nearest one. I kept the gun aimed at the tent at all times, just in case someone started shooting at me.

Chalky and Harry were doing a good job, with a constant stream of fire making sure the Italians' attention stayed on them. I wondered how much ammunition they had left.

I looked out from under the other side of the lorry towards the fuel dump. George was crouched down behind the drums of petrol. It wasn't exactly the safest hiding place; one bullet and he'd go up with nothing left of him but ashes. George saw me under the lorry and he gestured at two cans of petrol he'd got hold of. I gave him a thumbs-up.

George pointed at the tent where the shooting was coming from and then held up three fingers. So there were three of them in there with their guns aimed at the open area. I guessed they wouldn't shoot at George while he was in cover behind the fuel drums. They'd kill him all right, but they'd also lose all their fuel and risk blowing themselves up in the process. I was hoping that all their attention would be concentrated on the fuel dump, waiting for George to come out on his return trip.

I inched forwards on my stomach from under the cover of the lorry and worked my way flat on the sand, holding the gun in front of me, towards the tent. Chalky and Harry maintained their constant firing from the tank, keeping the other Italians' attention on them. I worked my way round to just in front of the flap of the tent, trying not to make any noise. Then I got to my feet, expecting at any second a burst of gunfire.

I looked across to George's position but I couldn't see him now, he was hidden behind the fuel drums. I hoped he'd be listening and would know that when I started shooting it was the signal for him to make his move. I checked the gun one last time, then I fired at just above ground level through the canvas of the tent. After a few seconds I took a quick look inside. They'd been caught by surprise. My burst had hit them low and all three of them were lying on the ground, groaning and clutching their legs.

Out of the corner of my eye I saw George start his run, a can of petrol hanging from each hand, and I began to cover the tents with my machine-gun, moving backwards all the time, heading for the lorries. The firing from Bessie carried on, CHATTERCHATTER-CHATTERCHATTERCHATTER as Harry and Chalky fired on.

I rolled back under the lorry again and paused before sprinting back to the tank, firing all the time. George ran round to the back of Bessie, to the fuel tank.

I clambered up on to the front compartment and dropped back into my driver's seat. I was sweating like pig. It wasn't just the heat, it was the fear.

Harry and Chalky kept up their firing for the few minutes it took for George to get the petrol into Bessie's tank, then the sound of George's boots scraping on the hull and the clang of the hatch dropping back into place told me we were ready.

'Right, Smith!' snapped Weston. 'Get us out of here!'

I started Bessie up and moved her back. After we'd gone about a hundred yards, Weston ordered me to halt. He gave orders to George and Harry.

'Four medium shells into the camp,' he said. 'Destroy all their remaining vehicles so they can't follow us.'

We heard Harry and George load their medium guns and open fire. We watched as the lorries blew up and caught fire, the fire spreading to the tents. The surviving Italian soldiers ran out from behind the burning cover, yelling and shouting, throwing caution to the winds. This was too much for them. They held their hands above their heads in surrender, afraid that next we'd hit them.

'They're surrendering, sir,' I said.

'Good,' said Weston. 'We'll lock them up in their own compound. Then we'll take whatever fuel and ammunition we can carry. We've got a long way to go before we get home.'

Chapter 13
Under Attack

It didn't take us long to herd the few remaining Italians into their own compound and lock the gates. They'd be able to climb the wire and get out, but it would take them time. And the more time we had, the better it was for us.

We loaded some more fuel drums on to the back of Bessie's hull and replenished our stock of ammunition – both sizes of shells for the bigger guns and bullets for the machine-guns – before setting off again.

It had been nearly two hours since the two Australians had staged the fight that had signalled the start of the mass escape. The lorries taking them had long gone. It was our hope that they'd been able to get back to our own lines and let our side know what had happened. As Weston said, we were a long way from home, behind enemy lines, and we could do with some help if we ran into the Axis forces on our way.

We drove in silence for a while. I took a quick look at Chalky. He still looked a bit ill. With one hand I disconnected my throat mike, then reached out and disconnected his. Chalky looked at me, surprised, but I didn't want to make him feel worse with the other lads listening to what we had to say.

'Feeling sick?' I asked.

He nodded. 'It's not the same when you kill them from a tank,' he said. 'You don't see them. They're just . . . just so far away. But when you actually see them up close, lying there, and you know that you've killed someone's husband, someone's brother, it's terrible.'

'I know it's awful, but it's them or us, Chalky,' I replied.

'I'll be OK,' he said. 'I'll just keep telling myself, "They're dropping bombs on my mum", and I'll be all right. Thanks, John.'

I reconnected my throat mike and gestured for Chalky to do the same.

We were all quiet in the tank after that, keeping our thoughts to ourselves and looking out for anything on the horizon. Every so often Prof would send out a radio call, hoping that he'd make contact, but with no luck. All around us the desert was empty. Empty and silent.

Bessie was a tank without markings because the Italians had never got round to painting on their colours. If anyone spotted us, she was a tank without a country.

We must have been travelling for about two hours when we heard a plane. Weston, in the open turret, took a sighting. Then he dropped down into the tank and shut the hatch.

'A Stuka,' he announced over the intercom. 'Full speed ahead, Smith.'

We were already going as fast as we could, but I tried to get a little more out of her, knowing that we were about to be bombed by a Stuka.

The dive bomber came low over us, checking us out. The lack of symbols obviously puzzled the pilot at first, but not for long. The Stuka turned and came back towards us, this time in a firing position.

'Gun up,' ordered Weston.

George elevated the main gun as best he could, but it's almost impossible to get the right elevation for an attacking plane. The Stuka flew over us, giving us a burst with its guns as it passed over, the bullets ricocheting off our armoured hull and turret.

'Zigzag, Smith,' ordered Weston.

I had been thinking of doing just that, anyway. A plane gets a line of fire to set up its bombing run. By zigzagging you can keep away from the straight bombing line, providing your tank can turn very tightly.

I began to zigzag, turning sharply to the left and then accelerating away, just as we heard the Stuka turn and come back at us from behind. I swung to the right and then to the left again. I had been lucky in the way I'd chosen. The Stuka dropped its first bomb, but it exploded away to our right and a massive shower of sand rained down on us. Too close for comfort.

We heard the drone of the Stuka's engine as it flew on. Then we saw it bank ahead of us as it turned into position for its next bombing run.

I could hear Prof urgently sending out call signs over the radio. I didn't pay much attention to what he was saying; I was concentrating on keeping Bessie moving backwards and forwards, then moving straight, before turning and zigzagging, as I tried to throw the Stuka off getting a firm sighting on us. Chalky, George and Harry opened up with their Brownings as the plane came in for its dive, doing their best to put the pilot off. The Stuka's second bomb smashed into the desert barely fifty yards away. He'd missed – but only just.

'He's getting closer,' I said.

'You're doing well, Smith,' said Weston over my headphones. 'Keep it up.'

I put Bessie through another turn . . . and then disaster struck! We ground to a halt!

'Smith!' yelled Weston. 'What's happened?'

I revved up the engine, but Bessie wouldn't move and just sank deeper into the sand.

'I think we've hit soft sand, sir!' I yelled.

Behind us we heard the Stuka turn, flying higher now to make sure that when he came in this time he was out of range of the machine-guns. Frantically I pulled at the levers, stamped on the pedals, but to no avail. We just lurched backwards and forwards, literally stuck in a rut, while the Stuka came in for the kill on a sitting target.

Harry and George swung their guns towards the oncoming plane and hammered away, but it was useless: the Stuka had chosen its height carefully. This was like the last time, only worse. Everyone dead and all because I was a useless tank driver.

'Get us out of here, Smith!' bellowed Weston.

I started to panic as Bessie rocked uselessly on the spot . . . and then suddenly I knew what we had to do. It was an insane idea, but the only chance we had.

'Drop the main gun and fire into the sand, George!' I yelled.

'What?' demanded George, bewildered.

'Don't argue, just do it!' I yelled.

There was a shell already in the breech. George swung the gun down as low as it would go and fired. As I felt the gun fire, I kicked Bessie into reverse and with the recoil we rocked backwards out of the sand hole. Immediately I swung Bessie part-way round and carried on reversing at speed, just as the Stuka let fly with its bomb. It landed and exploded in exactly the place where just ten seconds earlier we'd been trapped. Once again, we were covered in sand, but we had survived.

'Brilliant, John!' laughed Prof.

'Well done, Smith,' complimented Weston. 'But we're not out of danger yet. Here he comes again!'

The Stuka turned for its final attack. This time we also heard the sounds of more aircraft approaching, and my heart sank.

'He's called up reinforcements,' came Harry's voice. 'We're finished now!'

As we watched, the other planes grew larger in the sky. I could see six of them. But their wing-shapes were different. They weren't Stukas.

'They're ours!' called out Harry excitedly.

He was right. Two of the planes flew out of the formation and headed for the Stuka that was coming straight for us again. The German pilot saw them coming and turned, but not before he had released his final bomb at us. Fortunately this distraction had spoiled the bomber's aim and the bomb exploded some distance behind us.

Then the two Allied planes opened fire and we saw the Stuka take a hit. Thick black smoke poured out from its engine. It hung in the sky for a second before spinning and tumbling out of the sky, followed by an enormous explosion as it crashed into the desert a couple of miles away from us.

By now Prof was jabbering away on the radio, talking to the lead pilot of the formation. Then he relayed his conversation to

Weston, and we all heard it.

'We're back behind our own lines, sir!' he said excitedly. 'The Germans and Italians have been pushed back from Alamein! We're winning!'

We all burst into cheering. We'd done it!

'Chaps,' said Weston's cheerful voice over my headphones, 'it looks like we're home!'

Chapter 14
Home

As we neared our own front line we passed burnt-out German and Italian tanks and the ruins of Axis machine-gun posts. Barbed wire and debris were strewn around all over the place. The Axis positions had been hammered and overrun. Behind us the Germans and Italians were now in retreat. Weston stood up in the open hatch, a make-shift Union flag we'd found tied to the radio aerial, flying alongside him.

We passed a few divisions of our own troops moving forward, foot soldiers backed up by tanks and armoured cars. Then more soldiers and more tanks and more armoured cars. The Eighth Army was on the move, advancing just as Monty had promised.

'Maybe we ought to turn round and go the same way as everyone else, sir?' suggested George.

'We will soon enough,' grinned Weston. 'Once we've reported back to our unit and let them know we're safe and ready to resume action.'

'Resume action, sir?' grinned Harry. 'I didn't realize we'd stopped!'

We were all laughing at Harry's joke, when an open car came heading straight towards us, flashing its headlights at us to stop. I eased on the brake and brought Bessie to a halt. The car pulled up right in front of us, and a major climbed out from the back and stood staring at Bessie.

'What is this tank doing out of uniform?' he demanded.

We all tried not to laugh out loud. Weston was the only one who kept a straight face.

'It's a rather long story, sir,' he said.

He was just starting to tell the major about our adventures, when another car appeared, a cloud of sand and dust trailing behind it. Immediately the major sprang to attention and saluted, as did Weston. The second car pulled up and down from it stepped Monty himself.

'At ease!' ordered Monty crisply.

All around us, everyone had stopped. All vehicles, all foot soldiers, everything. Everyone was watching Monty as he surveyed Bessie. Weston dropped down from the hatch on to the sand and saluted.

'Lieutenant Weston and Tank Crew 247 reporting for duty, sir!' he said.

'Good,' said Monty.

Monty studied Bessie for a moment, noticing the painted-out insignia and the marks of damage. Then he came round to the driver's hatch and looked at me. I saluted as best I could from my position, and I thought I saw a twinkle in his eye.

'Driver Smith,' said Monty, 'we meet again. I see you are in possession of an unusual tank. Stolen?'

'No, sir,' I replied. 'It's ours. We recaptured it from the Italians and brought it back. We thought it might come in handy!'

Behind Monty's back, the major looked like he was about to turn purple in the face with anger. Monty gave a little smile.

'Quite right,' he said. 'From now on we're going to need all the tanks we can get! We're going on to victory!'

With that, he turned to the major and said: 'I want every one of these men in this tank recommended for military honours. These are the kind of men I want in my army. Give me men like these and we'll win this war. Heroes, every one. Make a note of their names.'

The major swallowed, astonished at this sudden turn of events. Then he saluted.

'Yes, sir,' he said.

'Good,' said Monty crisply. 'Carry on.'

Monty strode back to his car, got in and drove off.

The major stood looking at us for a few seconds, still unable to come to terms with what he had just seen and heard, then he turned to his adjutant and ordered: 'You heard the C-in-C, Brownlow. Get their names. They're heroes.'

And when they heard those words, all the men standing around, whether on foot, or in jeeps or in tanks, began to cheer and came over to shake our hands. Crew 247 had come home.

Alamein and After

John Smith's story was set during the period of the Battle of El Alamein. In fact, this was a series of battles which lasted from July 1942 until early November 1942. After a number of fierce attacks and counter-attacks by both sides around the area of El Alamein, the Allies finally broke out in November 1942, forcing the Axis forces to retreat.

During November and December 1942 the Eighth Army advanced from El Alamein to El Agheila, pushing the Axis forces back. This was the first occasion in the desert war when the Germans had been in retreat for such a length of time. The retreat by the Axis forces went on right through the winter and into the spring of 1943.

The Allied advance continued up to May 1943, with the German forces fighting all the way in their forced retreat across North Africa. Towards the end of this campaign the Eighth Army was joined by American and French forces of United States II Corps, following a sea-landing. Finally, the end of all Axis resistance in North Africa came on 12 May. The war in the North African desert was over.

The Significance of Alamein

Up until the victory at Alamein, the Allies had been losing the Second World War. The victory at Alamein had a three-fold effect:

• It showed that the might of the German army could be defeated, and in this way raised morale throughout the rest of the Allied forces.

• It secured the Suez Canal for the Allies as a vital supply line.

• It led directly to the successful Italian campaign, with Montgomery's forces and the American forces under General Mark Clark moving on from North Africa to conquer Italy, forcing the Italians to surrender.

Alamein: Rommel v. Montgomery

Panzerarmee Afrika

50,000 German, 54,000 Italian **104,000**

211 German – 85 Mark IIIs, 88 Mark III Specials,
        8 Mark IVs, 30 Mark IV Specials
278 Italian, mainly M13/40s **489**

475 Field and medium = 200 German, 275 Italian
744 Anti-tank = 444 German (86 = 8.8cm, 68 = 7.62cm, 290 = 5.0cm)
        300 Italian **1,219**

275 German (150 serviceable), 400 Italian (200 serviceable) **675**

Eighth Army

195,000

170 Grants, 252 Shermans, 216 Crusader 2-pounders
78 Crusader 6-pounders, 119 Stuarts, 194 Valentines

1,029

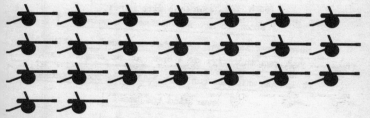

908 Field and medium
1,403 Anti-tank = 554 2-pounders, 849 6-pounders

2,311

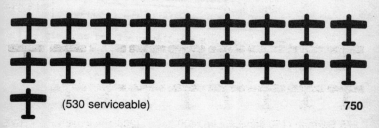

(530 serviceable)

750

Excerpts from Tank Tip

Drawn up by Col. Ernest Swinton, founder of the Heavy Section, Machine Gun Corps, in 1916, and still in use for tank crews in the Second World War.

Remember your orders

Shoot quick

Shoot low. A miss which throws dust in the enemy's eyes is better than one that whistles in his ear.

Shoot cunning.

Shoot the enemy while they are rubbing their eyes. Economize ammunition and don't kill a man three times.

Watch the progress of the fight and your neighbouring tanks. Watch the infantry whom you are helping.

Remember the position of your own line.

One 6pdr shell that hits the loophole of a machine-gun emplacement will do it in.

Use the 6pdr with care: shoot to hit and not make a noise.

Never have any gun, even when unloaded, pointing at your own infantry; or a 6pdr gun at another tank.

It is the unloaded gun that kills the fool's friends.

Never mind the heat.

Never mind the noise.

Never mind the dust.

Think of your pals in the infantry.

Thank God you are bullet proof and can help the infantry, who are not.

Allies Advance

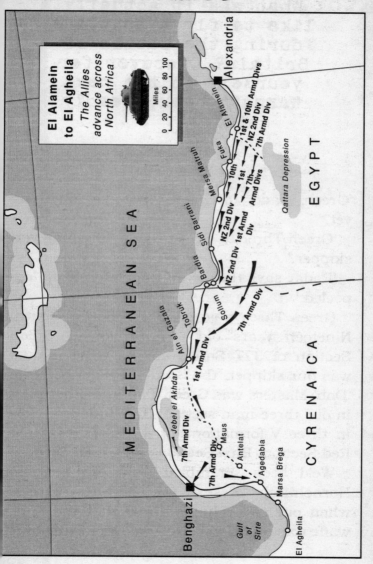

El Alamein to El Agheila

The Allies advance across North Africa

Miles
0 20 40 60 80 100

What was it actually
like to fly a Spitfire
during the Battle of
Britain? Discover for
yourself in the next
Warpath book, *Deadly
Skies* . . .

'Green Leader to Green Three, see anything yet?'

'Green Three to Green Leader. Nothing yet, skipper.'

'Radar says they're on their way. Keep 'em peeled.'

Green Three was me, John 'Bonzo' Smith. Nineteen years old. Third pilot in Green Section of 327 Squadron. Ian 'Tug' Banks was our skipper, the Section Leader. Charlie 'Dob' Masters was Green Two, the other pilot in our three-man section. 327 Squadron flew in three V-formations of three planes each: Red Section, Blue Section and Green Section.

We'd been scrambled from our base in Hornchurch, Essex, five minutes earlier, when our radar had warned that the Luftwaffe was on its way. Now we were flying over north Kent, just to the east of London. Below me I could see the mud flats of the Thames estuary, the river now wide and merging with the sea – cold and blue, so very different from the thin brown river that snaked through London.

'Still no sign.'

'Let's take a stroll and see what we can find,' came the voice of Jerry Payne, the leader of Red Section, in my headphones.

He took a turn to the right, and one by one each section followed him, spreading out so that we patrolled the east Kent area in a line formation.

I was relatively new to Spitfires. I'd joined 327 Squadron just two months earlier after my training, most of which had been done on Tiger Moths and Miles Masters. Compared to the Tiger and the Miles, the Spitfire was more cramped, but I soon learned the benefits of its slim design. The narrower Spitfire was able to turn much quicker and get you out of trouble when under attack. It was able to twist and turn, loop and dive in a short arc, providing you could take the strain that came with a sudden loss of gravity as you dived, or the increased pressure as you went into a steep climb. Even after two months I still felt excitement when at the controls of a Spitfire, surely the best fighter plane in the whole world!

Suddenly I saw the enemy planes approaching at 17,000 feet, about half a mile ahead of us: sixteen Messerschmitt Me-109s, instantly recognizable by their yellow nose-tips, flying in the German 'finger-four' formations.

'Here we go!' came Red Leader's voice over my headphones. 'Battle formations.'